The Fine Print

The Fine Print

A Novel

Cheri J. Crane

Covenant Communications, Inc.

Published by Covenant Communications, Inc.
American Fork, Utah
Copyright © 1995 by Cheri J. Crane
All rights reserved
Printed in the United States of America
First Printing: August 1995
01 00 99 98 97 96 95 94 10 9 8 7 6 5 4 3 2 1

Library of Congress Cataloging-in-Publication Data
Crane, Cheri J. (Cheri Jackson), 1961-
The Fine Print: a novel / Cheri J. Crane.
ISBN 1-55503-837-9
I. Title.
PS3553.R2696P75   1995
813'.54—dc20   95-4810
                              CIP

For Kennon. Thanks for interpreting the fine print.

Acknowledgments

I'd like to thank my editors, JoAnn Jolley and Valerie Holladay, for the suggestions and guidance that improved the initial concept. Thanks also to everyone else at Covenant!

To my sons, Kris, Derek, and Devin: thanks for your patience, help, and willingness to share your mother. And to Kennon—thanks for all you do.

Thanks also to Denise Kallstrom, Michelle Martineau, Lin Phelps, and the other members of the Bear Lake Chapter of the American Diabetic Association (ADA), whose friendship and experiences gave this book diabetic insight. May we continue in our daily quest to live the good life.

A debt of gratitude is extended to Dr. John Liljenquist—an inspiring physician, endocrinologist, internist, and diabetologist—and to Christine T. Nelson—a diabetic counselor and talented R.N., for the education received under your expert tutelage. Also my appreciation to those wonderful people at the Rocky Mountain Diabetes Diagnostic and Treatment Center: Bobbi, Lisa, Annette, Marjorie, Paula, Sharee, Stuart, Merodene, Joyce, Vicki, Stephanie, Cynthia, Becky, and Robert. (I hope I didn't miss anybody.) Thanks for all you do!!!

Special thanks should also go to Jan Albertson, Janette Mecham, and Jocelyn Nield for your patience in explaining how the new Primary concept works . . . most of the time.

Finally, a big thank you to Shelley, Melissa, and Angela Burdick for the hours of proofreading, the helpful hints, and the encouragement that aided in the completion of this novel.

To all of you: "Merci beaucoup!" Or, as we say in my household, mercy buckets!

Prologue

Some women compare weight or dress sizes. Some kid each other about hair color. With Sally and me, it was blood sugar levels. We were always giving each other a bad time, rubbing it in if one of us was closer to the normal range than the other. As diabetics, we didn't always follow the rules. We tried—on occasion—but with so much around to enjoy and savor, we took lightly the threats of kidney failure, heart disease, nerve damage and blindness. Those things happened to other people, not us.

Sally was only ten when her parents learned she was diabetic. My own body didn't start deteriorating until I was fourteen. I met Sally seven years ago in an internist's office in Idaho Falls. As we exchanged jokes, waiting for our turn to the see the doctor, it became apparent that we possessed the same warped sense of humor. It didn't take long for the two of us to become close friends. We attended concerts and plays (two things our husbands despised), went shopping together, offered moral support if one of us succumbed to the torment of exercise, and even scheduled doctor appointments for the same day, teaming up for frequent episodes of diabetic rebellion.

Since we had both felt the cloud of doom hanging over our heads for so long, we were determined to ignore it. Our binges were relatively infrequent, but there were a few times when a craving for something sweet overwhelmed our good intentions. We ate a cookie here, a tiny sliver of cake there, convinced it was "good therapy." Because we couldn't see the risks involved, they didn't exist—the ostrich approach to life.

Living with diabetes is like walking a tight rope—perfect balance is difficult to maintain. Slips can be dangerous, even fatal.

Sally and I refused to let exercise, diet, and tight control become the center of our lives.

Many diabetics live long, productive lives. Research has handed us tools that make life bearable. Taking it seriously is the first step toward gaining control of an otherwise volatile situation. Everything affects a diabetic's blood sugar level—exercise, illness, stress—and for women, pregnancy rates as one of the greater challenges.

Surprisingly, Sally sailed through her first pregnancy with relatively few complications. We both adored her daughter, Brook, who eventually learned to call me Auntie Teri. Being around Sally's bubbly daughter started me thinking about having a child of my own—despite the risks. But Sally's second pregnancy changed my mind. Unlike the first, it wasn't planned. Her monthly cycle had always been irregular, so it failed to serve as a red flag. She didn't experience the nausea she suffered during her first pregnancy, and she wasn't suspicious until she began gaining weight. Panic-stricken, she and her husband, Gerald, rushed to see her physician, who told her she was nearly three months pregnant.

Diabetics are told to keep their diet and blood sugars under tight control during a pregnancy, as the weeks before and during the first trimester of the gestational period are vital to the baby's health. Knowing it might be too late for the infant's health, Sally struggled to bring her blood sugars down, but the pregnancy was difficult. Despite her efforts and those of the medical profession, the baby was stillborn. Because of the extra strain on her body, two months later, Sally suffered a heart attack and passed quietly out of my life.

It was a time of sorrow, rage, and shock. As the weeks passed, I tried to deal with the loss, though it was difficult to believe that someone as vibrant as Sally was gone. After a few months, Sally's husband, Gerald, took five-year-old Brook and moved to Oregon to live with his parents. I understood his reasons for leaving, and I grieved for the tiny girl who would now grow up without her mother.

Hardly a day goes by that I don't think about Sally. She was easily one of the best friends I've ever had. I doubt anyone will ever take her place.

Chapter 1

Normally, I accept callings without hesitation, but this time when the powers that be summoned me into the bishop's office, I balked. I sensed I wasn't going to like what they had to say and soon discovered I was right.

My first impulse was to say, "NO!" That was also my second, third, and fourth impulse. But, somehow, a "yes" slipped out from between my clenched teeth. It was habit, I suppose. Regardless, I was certain I hadn't done myself a favor. "That's not what I meant to say," I said, trying to rectify the situation.

"Sorry," Bishop Anderson said in that sweet voice he saves for people who are trying to wiggle out of an undesired calling. "We have it on record and in front of witnesses that you just agreed to accept this position."

"But . . . c'mon guys," I pleaded. The entire bishopric grinned like a group of Cheshire cats.

"We're glad you're taking this so well," Ed Bergen began.

I sent the second counselor a withering look. "I can't possibly serve in the Primary," I informed them. "I'm on a set schedule because of my diabetes. I have to eat lunch at—"

"Precisely twelve o'clock," Bishop Anderson said, interrupting my prepared speech. "Mark mentioned that earlier when we talked to him."

I made myself a mental note to thank my husband for his support. Always looking out for me, Mark had obviously emphasized the reasons that would keep me from serving in the Primary. Frankly, I was puzzled that I was being asked to accept this calling.

It wasn't like I had a choice. Since Primary in our ward was currently held from 11:30 p.m. till 1:10 p.m., I stayed home during Sunday School to give my insulin shot and eat lunch. I always showed up in time for Relief Society and Sacrament Meeting, putting a valiant effort into my current position as the ward chorister.

"We've got it all worked out," Bishop Anderson continued. "Sister Cox said the lunch thing would be no problem. Bring it to church. You can slip out and eat when you need to. As her first counselor, you'll have more freedom to take care of these . . . er . . . matters than if you were a teacher. We've given this a lot of thought and prayer and feel this *is* an inspired calling."

Frustrated, I ran a hand through my short, black hair. What were these people thinking? This wasn't inspiration—this was desperation! Not only were they asking me to put a calling before my health, but they were asking me to serve in an organization that catered to children. I knew it would be a painful reminder of the children I would never have. Their presence would also resurrect memories of Sally's little girl, Brook, inviting unwanted emotions to surface without warning.

Almost as bad was being asked to serve with a woman who set my teeth on edge—Natalie Cox. She was the image of a Molly Mormon. You know the type: beautiful, with perfect teeth and perfect hair. Mrs. Clean, whose house always smells like Lemon Pledge. I slumped in my chair and longed to scream. Instead, a quiet groan slipped out.

"Sister Patterson, are you all right?" Ed Bergen ventured, looking concerned.

At first, I refused to dignify the question with a reply. Then I wondered if I was onto something. I could fake going into insulin shock—something Sally and I had often joked about doing when we were in a tight spot. The bishopric would all feel so guilty that the Primary position would be forgotten. As I prepared to faint to the floor, an irritating inner voice began to nag. I knew I was licked. Once my conscience kicks in, there's no getting around it. The thing would pester me for days. The only plausible solution was to accept the calling and let everyone see for themselves the mistake they were making by placing me in the Primary. It wouldn't be long before they'd call me back into this very office to admit someone's spiritual radar had been off a few kilometers.

"Teri?" Bishop Anderson said softly.

"I'm fine," I replied. "A little surprised. I never thought—Anyway, that's not important right now. If I'm being called to this position, there must be a reason. I'll give it my best shot," I said brightly. The diabetic humor floated past their combined intellect.

The three men looked relieved as they rose to their feet to congratulate me. I thought sympathy would have been more in order, but, determined to appear cordial, I forced a grim smile. Bishop Anderson grinned as he enthusiastically pumped my hand. "I have a feeling this calling will bring numerous blessings into your life," he said, patting me on the shoulder. I nodded and left the room.

On the way home, I cranked up the radio, allowing my jumbled emotions to mingle freely with the classic rock that I usually listen to. Music has always been a magical balm for me, but it failed to work this time. Desperate, I tuned into a classical music station. As Chopin's Nocturne in E-Flat Major floated through the interior of my maroon Geo Prism, I tried once again to relax. Again, the music failed. I switched off the radio and stared in the rear view mirror. "Get a grip," I grumbled, focusing my eyes on the road ahead.

I drove in silence for nearly ten minutes, making my way through the Idaho Falls traffic. At last I turned down my street and pulled into the driveway, too preoccupied to give much thought to the unfamiliar car parked in front of the house. I pushed a button under the dash and impatiently waited for the garage door to open, then parked beside Mark's pride and joy, a full-size brown Blazer. I grabbed my purse, stepped out of the car, and stomped toward the house where I planned to unload on my unsuspecting husband.

I stormed inside, slammed my purse onto a kitchen counter and threw my keys beside it. "MARK!" I said loudly. "I want to talk to you, NOW! Quit hiding and come out here and take this like a man! How dare you give the bishopric permission to ruin my life!"

"Heh, heh, heh. That's my Teri. Always full of fun," Mark said, moving into view. Beside him stood Natalie Cox. I blinked. What was this, Pick-on-Teri-Day?

"Uh . . . hi . . . Teri," Natalie began awkwardly. "When Bishop Anderson called to say you'd accepted, I couldn't wait. I've been a nervous wreck all week. I was so excited, I had to come over and tell you how happy I am that you agreed to serve with me in the Primary. I know this will be a challenge for you," she stammered. "You don't know how I've struggled with this decision. But, I couldn't ignore the prompting . . . your name came to me so strongly . . ." She seemed to wilt before my eyes.

I could see that Mark was almost as upset with me as I was with him. Sighing, I walked around the bar and touched Natalie's shoulder. "It's all right," I said, "I was kidding. I'm really okay about this. See, I'm smiling," I added, forcing a smile.

Natalie returned the smile shyly. "It'll work out, you'll see," she said, putting her arms around me and pulling me close in a grateful hug. Silently, I fought for air. I'm not into hugs much, unless they're from Mark. In fact, I have a high need for personal space. Except for Sally, there aren't many people I've been comfortable with, and even fewer that I would let hug me. But I valiantly endured this one, sensing it was the least I could do. When she finally let me go, her smile was radiant. "I'll call you later," she said softly. She allowed Mark to guide her through the dining room, toward the living room and the front door. As they moved from view, I walked to the counter and sank onto a bar stool to sulk.

"Well, that was smooth," Mark commented a few minutes later.

"Don't push it, Mark," I warned. "I had no idea she was here."

"She was parked right out front," he countered, his brown eyes condemning me.

"I didn't see her car," I retorted, feeling close to tears myself.

Sensing the shape I was in, Mark held out his arms. I pouted for a few seconds, then slipped off the stool and had myself a nice cry on his shoulder.

Chapter 2

"So, should we divide the ten-year-old class?" Natalie asked. "Fourteen kids that age would be challenge to handle. Teri, what do you think? Teri?"

Startled out of my brief retreat into self-pity mode, I looked up. Edna Barrett, our newly called secretary, and Gloria Hansen, the new second counselor were both staring at me.

"Do you need something to eat, Teri, dear?" Edna asked, oozing with superior knowledge. The retired R.N. smiled kindly in a way that both repulses and annoys.

"No," I said, trying to keep the irritation I felt out of my voice.

"You're sure? A patient we had one time in the hospital, a *diabetic*," she stressed, "couldn't tell when he was in insulin shock. He gave us several scares."

"Teri, do you feel all right?" Natalie asked, her concerned blue eyes searching mine. "I mean, don't hesitate to let us know if you're ever . . . you know—"

"Natalie, you'd better get a glass of juice," Edna demanded, taking control of the situation. Startled with the urgency in Edna's voice, Natalie turned toward Edna, who nodded abruptly, causing her unnaturally dark curls to bounce furiously on top of her head.

"Should I call 911?" Gloria asked, her eyes wide with alarm. The young woman quickly rose from her chair and nervously flipped a strand of long red hair over one shoulder.

"We just need some juice here," Edna assured Gloria as she motioned for Natalie to flee to the kitchen.

I rolled my eyes and silently pleaded for help. Without divine intervention, I would explode.

"See, what did I tell you, Teri's eyes have rolled back in her head. Next thing, she'll be passing out," Edna said jubilantly. She quickly flew to my side and patted my arm. "Natalie, make it quick with that juice!" she commanded.

"Look, guys" I said, pulling away from Edna. "Let's get something straight. I am perfectly capable of telling when I'm in trouble with my blood sugar. I'm fine. I was daydreaming a minute ago, okay?! I knew this kind of thing would happen. This is never going to work. I'd tried to tell the bishop . . . I tried to tell Mark, but nobody would listen."

Edna pushed me back into place on the couch. "Go get that juice!" she barked to Natalie. "Diabetics get unreasonable and ornery when their blood sugar is dropping. Trust me, I know what I'm talking about," she said, patting me on the shoulder.

"So do I," I fumed as I reached for my purse and pulled out my trusty One Touch. "Watch this."

I pushed a button on the blood sugar monitoring machine, bringing it to life. The computer beeped a quiet greeting as I wedged a strip into place. I quickly pricked my finger and forced a drop of blood onto the strip. Edna seemed fascinated. Natalie continued to look worried, and Gloria's face drained of all color.

"Oh, my," Gloria stammered, sinking into the chair behind her. "I've never seen anyone do that to herself before," she said, holding a hand to her mouth. Wiping my finger on a piece of tissue that I'd salvaged from my purse, I waited impatiently as the monitor's countdown neared completion.

"See, it's normal, 135," I said, gazing with disdain at our resident nurse.

"One thirty-five *is* slightly elevated," Edna said with a frown as she retreated to the recliner and sat down, apparently washing her hands of her recalcitrant patient.

Natalie moved back to the couch and stared at my monitor. "Teri's blood sugar is too high?" she asked, glancing at Edna for confirmation.

"One thirty-five is excellent for me," I said, slightly exasperated.

"What's normal?" Natalie pressed.

"Yeah?" Gloria added weakly.

Only too happy to respond, Edna began to explain. "A Type I diabetic, like Teri here, is a person whose pancreas no longer functions normally. Unless of course they have the adult-onset—"

"Type II," I offered.

"Adult-onset variety," she continued implacably. "In that case, sometimes, even if the pancreas produces insulin, the body doesn't metabolize sugars well."

"But—" Natalie tried to interrupt.

"The pancreas, of course," Edna continued gleefully, "is a gland that furnishes our bodies with a substance called insulin."

"I think we understand that part already," Natalie interrupted, glancing at Gloria. Gloria nodded in agreement. "What we're confused about . . . that is, what we're wondering . . . what's Teri's blood sugar level supposed to be?"

"As I was saying," Edna said, displeased by the interruption, "a diabetic, like Teri here," she said, gesturing once again to me, "who has juvenile—"

"Type I," I corrected.

"Juvenile diabetes," Edna repeated, "has to inject insulin. When she doesn't give enough insulin or eats something she shouldn't, her levels get too high." She gave me a pained look before continuing, "And the normal range is 80 to 120." Edna finished triumphantly, looking pleased with herself.

"Teri has to give herself shots?" Gloria asked, her complexion pallid.

Edna nodded and began expounding on the fine art of injecting insulin. Suddenly, Gloria bolted from the living room. Rising to the occasion, Edna followed, delighted to be called into action once again.

"Teri, level with me," Natalie said. "Are you going to be all right?"

"Yes. From the sound of things, I'm in better shape than Gloria."

Natalie sighed, then shook her head. "I'm sorry if we . . . if Edna upset you. She comes on a little strong sometimes, but she means well." She flinched as Gloria began a vigorous session of dry heaves.

11

"Well, I'm definitely not the one we should be concerned about this morning," I replied, my feathers still a bit ruffled.

"Gloria will be all right. Another seven months and she'll be as good as new."

"Hmmm?" I said. The obvious went right past me.

"She's due in March."

"What?" I still didn't get it.

"Gloria's pregnant. Didn't you know?"

"Great," I muttered as I retrieved my One Touch from the mahogany coffee table.

"What was that?" Natalie murmured as she moved across her living room and glanced down the hall toward the bathroom.

"Uh . . . great," I said, trying to cover up. "How exciting for Gloria. And to think, she's only been married six months." I shoved the monitor into my purse and picked up the notebook I'd brought with me.

"You don't have to leave now?" Natalie asked with alarm.

I shrugged and glanced down the hall. Gloria stood quietly before Edna, who was still barking orders.

"Gloria will be fine," Natalie said with a smile. "Edna wants me to get her a cup of herbal tea. She can sip at it while we finish planning."

I had to give the woman credit. Natalie was trying so hard. Not only had she obviously picked Edna as the secretary to handle any medical emergencies I might throw their way, but she was so willing to accommodate our individual quirks that it was nauseating. I decided it would be best to leave before I joined Gloria in that already over-populated room down the hall. Sliding my purse onto my shoulder, I said, "Sorry, Natalie. I have to work this afternoon, and there's so much I need to do before I—"

"Oh. Well, maybe tomorrow . . ."

"I meant what I said earlier. This isn't going to work. I know I told the bishop I'd try, but—"

"Teri, please."

I really tried to avoid that imploring face. I even turned my head, but suddenly, the woman had moved directly in front of me.

"I know this will be a challenge for all of us. Maybe we didn't

12

handle things right today, but you have to understand, we were concerned. And when Edna—"

"It's not just Edna," I quietly replied, certain she would never understand why I wanted to desert my post. "Although I think we both know why she was called to be secretary."

Natalie looked away, but I saw the tears glistening in her eyes. "I won't force you into this, Teri. It's your choice. All I know is how I felt each time I prayed about your name. But there's only so much I can do. The rest is up to you."

I scowled at the spotless carpet. If the woman had hit me with anything else, I could've argued my way out of it. Natalie Cox didn't play fair. The funny thing was, I admired her for it. It's the same strategy I often use on Mark. Playing the role of the wounded victim, laying on the guilt. Implying that he really has a choice. I sighed and replaced my purse on the coffee table. "Okay, you win," I said, my voice barely audible.

"Really?" Natalie looked up at me hopefully.

I returned her delighted stare with a look of disgust. The tears had disappeared without a trace from those baby blues. What an actress this woman was!

"You'll never regret this," she promised, sealing my lack of enthusiasm with a suffocating hug. I gasped for air until she finally pulled away to wipe at her eyes. "I promise to tell Edna to give you some space," she said with a smile. "We'll assume you're all right unless you tell us otherwise."

I nodded and forced a smile that was closer to a grimace.

"Natalie, is the tea ready?" Edna demanded.

"Not quite," Natalie replied, winking at me before she hurried from the room, calling behind her. "It's coming right up." I sank onto the couch, rested my chin on my hands, and wondered why I'd agreed to stick this out. It didn't make sense. I'd had a chance to bail and had blown it.

"Natalie, you'd better grab some juice for Teri. She's looking a little peaked," Edna said as she marched out of the living room.

Looking toward heaven, I wondered if Sally had a bird's eye view to this humiliation. *I could do it if you were here*, I said to her silently. What a difference a true friend makes.

13

"Teri, it couldn't have been as bad as you're making it sound."

I picked up a sofa pillow from the love seat and threw it at Mark. He caught it with ease and added it to the one under his head as he stretched out on the couch.

"It was horrible, Mark. You don't know. You weren't there."

"Sounds like I missed quite a performance," he said with a grin. "Edna the Super Nurse, in action once again."

"Edna the Terrible, you mean," I countered.

"Teri . . ." His tone was placating, which irritated me no end.

"That woman is dangerous! I shudder to think what would have happened if Natalie hadn't run interference."

"I'm sure Edna was just trying to help."

"Maybe, but there's so much she doesn't understand about the current treatment for diabetes."

"She means well," Mark interrupted.

I sighed heavily. "Natalie said the same thing."

"Well, it's true. Edna worked as a nurse for years. In fact, if I'm not mistaken, she was there when I made my grand entrance into this world."

"That explains a few things," I replied. "She probably let you fall out onto the floor."

"Not funny," he informed me. "Edna Barrett helped a lot of people over the years. She was the best!"

"Emphasis on *was*," I added drily.

Mark sat up and gave me a dirty look. "Edna's life hasn't exactly been easy, you know. Her husband was killed in a railroad accident years ago. She raised those two boys of hers alone."

"Now, there's a real mystery," I pondered innocently. "I can't imagine why a woman like that stayed single."

"Teri!"

I shook my head. "Give it up, Mark. You'll never convince me Edna Barrett is anything but a royal pain!"

Mark crossed the room and pulled me up from the love seat. "Promise me one thing."

"Depends on what it is," I replied, wiggling my eyebrows.

"That you'll treat your fellow Primary workers with the same consideration you expect from them."

I pulled a face.

"Teri . . ."

"Oh, all right," I groaned.

"Good girl," he said, leaning forward to kiss me. Slowly we eased onto the love seat as Mark did his best to help me forget about my very bad day.

Chapter 3

Sunday had arrived. I sat beside Mark in the chapel and fought the nervousness that was elevating my blood sugar level. A recent check had revealed I was at 287. Edna would be thrilled. *She'll never find out*, I vowed. To ensure this, I slipped down the hall and into the rest room to give myself a small shot of insulin.

Several minutes later, I walked up the carpeted steps that led to the pulpit in the front of the chapel. I had spent the entire week trying to decide on the hymns we would be singing today and had settled on "Master, the Tempest Is Raging" for the opening hymn. As I opened my hymn book to the correct page, I ignored the smirk on Mark's face. I knew he was thinking of the titles he had *helpfully* suggested all week. "Let Us All Press On." "Put Your Shoulder to the Wheel," and his personal favorite, "Be Still, My Soul."

I looked out over the congregation, glancing briefly at Natalie Cox, Edna Barrett, and Gloria Hansen—three women who were now a part of my life, despite my protests and misgivings. I tried to shake off the despair that came with that thought and concentrated on the hymn. The music began.

"Master the tempest is raging! The billows are tossing high!
The sky is o'ershadowed with blackness. No shelter or help is nigh."

As I sang the words, a strange thickness afflicted my throat. I forced it down with a swallow and continued to sing.

"Carest thou not that we perish? How canst thou lie asleep
When each moment so madly is threat'ning a grave in the angry deep?"

The realization that I was giving up a calling I loved for one I knew I was going to hate descended upon me with relentless fury. As my voice began to waver, I mouthed the words to the chorus, then did my best to join in on the second verse.

"Master, with anguish of spirit I bow in my grief today.

The depths of my sad heart are troubled. Oh, waken and save, I pray!"

I sang the last sentence with such fervor that even Mark looked alarmed. Somewhat subdued, I made it through the rest of the verse and subsequent chorus. Taking a deep breath, I prepared for the onslaught of the third verse. Why had I sabotaged myself with this particular hymn? I'd always tried to select the hymns prayerfully. As I'd thumbed through the index, this one had leaped off the page at me. Now, here it was, betraying emotions that were running too close to the surface.

"Master, the terror is over. The elements sweetly rest.

Earth's sun in the calm lake is mirrored, and heaven's within my breast."

A deep, penetrating calm began to spread throughout my body. Once again, I could only mouth the rest of the verse. Determined to make it through the chorus, I forced myself to sing.

"The winds and the waves shall obey thy will: Peace be still, peace be still.

Whether the wrath of the storm-tossed sea—Or demons or men or whatever it be,

No waters can swallow the ship where lies—The Master of ocean and earth and skies.

They all shall sweetly obey thy will: Peace be still; peace, be still."

My voice trembled on the last refrain. I looked down into the audience and saw that tears were racing down Natalie's face. Even Gloria appeared to be dabbing at her eyes. I glanced at Edna, who was frantically rummaging through her purse.

"They all shall sweetly obey thy will: Peace, peace, be still."

I closed the hymn book, my heart still warmed by a feeling of inner peace. I now knew that for some mysterious reason, I was needed in the Primary organization. Smiling, I stepped down from the stand and sat beside Mark on the front padded bench. As he slid an arm around my shoulders, Edna breathlessly appeared in front of us. I could feel the entire ward staring as she shoved a candy bar into my hand.

"Here, eat this before you fall on your head," she commanded in a loud whisper that everyone could overhear. "You were up there shaking like a leaf. I said to myself, 'Edna, that poor girl is going to pass out, right here in front of us!'"

I could have crawled in a hole. Instead I avoided the look I was getting from Bishop Anderson and the man who was waiting impatiently to offer the opening prayer. They stared down at us, watching as I tried to convince Edna that I didn't need the mashed Almond Joy clutched in her first. Finally I gripped her arm and led her out of the chapel, monitor in hand to prove my point.

When we returned, I tried to inconspicuously walk to my seat as Edna got in a parting shot.

"Two hundred and ten!" she snapped. "That girl's on the verge of a coma!" Holding her head high, she returned to her seat, convinced she had valiantly come to my rescue. I frowned and tried to ignore Mark's stifled laughter.

When the acting Primary presidency was officially relieved of duty, I could sense the curiosity buzzing throughout the congregation. Who would take the place of these four formidable women who had served so valiantly for the past three years? Mark gave me an intense squeeze. "You're going to do just fine," he encouraged.

When our names were announced, we stood, one by one, solemnly looking at each other. The sustaining vote confirmed that we were indeed the next Primary presidency. I met Natalie's questioning gaze with a smile. It was obvious that she had been afraid Edna's earlier outburst would push me over the edge again. It might have if I hadn't finally received the prompting that this calling was from the Lord.

The outgoing presidency took the remainder of the time to share their testimonies, and the various experiences that had convinced them the Primary was the most important organization in the Church. The closing hymn I had chosen was "Because I Have Been Given Much." After the closing prayer, Natalie hurried forward to gather me up in an intense hug. This time, I didn't mind.

The bishopric set us apart that night. First Natalie, then me, then Gloria, and finally, Edna. We were all promised we would develop a deep and abiding love for the children we would be working with. Natalie was given an added promise that she would find the patience and strength to deal with the challenges at home. I wondered at this. To the best of my knowledge, Natalie was already the most organized woman in the ward. I had no doubts she would come through with flying colors, with or without the extra blessing.

Edna was told this calling would bring great joy and satisfaction into her life. Gloria was promised health and strength, the two things I had hoped would be mentioned in my own blessing. Instead, I was assured I would grow spiritually and be a source of strength and support to the others. I was also promised that children would be coming into my home. I figured this one out later with Mark as we drove home.

"I've got it!" I said, pretending to be a sport about the wayward blessing. Those so-called words of inspiration had rubbed salt in a very sensitive wound.

"Got what?" Mark asked distantly. He'd been strangely quiet since I'd been set apart.

"That bit about children coming into our home. I know what Ed Bergen meant by that."

"Teri, that was inspiration coming from our Heavenly Father, not Ed Bergen."

"Yeah, whatever. Anyway," I added brightly, "I've figured it out. Those children coming into our home, they're your sister's kids. Remember, they'll be coming into our home for Thanksgiving!"

"Teri—"

"What?"

"I think there's more to it than that."

"Oh, right!" I replied, my voice oozing sarcasm.

Mark had finally caught on that I wasn't as cheerful as I had been trying to sound and reached across the gear shift to cover my hand with his. "That new internist you've been seeing, Dr. Molting—"

"You mean Moulton?"

"Yeah. Last month he said if we're very careful . . ." He left the sentence hanging in the air.

Not again, I thought to myself. I tried to speak calmly. "Mark, we've already been through this. You know diabetics run a high risk of having children with birth defects, not to mention the havoc a pregnancy can wreak with the diabetic's own health."

"It doesn't always turn out that way."

"What about Sally?"

Mark said nothing at first. A few minutes later, as he turned the Blazer into our driveway, he began, "What happened to Sally— "

"Could happen to me," I interrupted sharply.

"Teri," Mark said, "I know losing Sally hurt. She was a good friend."

It hurt too much to reply.

"Tell you what," Mark said softly. "We'll leave it in the Lord's hands." He slid close to hold me. I longed to cry, but the tears wouldn't come. I knew once I started, I would never stop.

Chapter Four

Natalie, Gloria, Edna, and I met together frequently in the days that followed. As time passed, I found that working with these women wasn't actually as bad as I had anticipated. True, Natalie exhibited an annoying fetish for cleanliness, but she was sincerely sweet. Gloria was young and inexperienced, but she possessed a wacky sense of humor that was rapidly making up for it. Edna was still a thorn in my side, but I was getting used to her pushy good intentions. Together we made a pretty good team.

The world of Primary had changed since I'd had anything to do with it. It took a while for me to catch on that some classes had been given different names. There were no Stars, Blazers, or Merrie Misses. Nursery through the three-year-olds were all known as Sunbeams. Four-year-olds through seven-year-olds were known as CTRs. That left the eight-year-olds through the eleven-year-olds, who were called Valiants. It was an adjustment—one of several I would have to make.

By Thursday, we were able to turn in our prospective list of teachers. A few modifications were later made, but as a whole, the bishopric tried to be supportive. We still lacked a teacher for the eleven-year-old Valiant boys, but the others were quickly called to their new positions. We would officially take the helm with our new organization on Sunday. I could hardly wait.

We had decided to start with everyone gathering into the Primary room for Opening Exercises, which would last precisely ten minutes. This was the schedule we had painstakingly worked out:

11:30 - 11:40 Opening exercises (10 min.)

11:40 - 11:45 Separate Sr. from Jr. Primary (5 min.)

11:45 - 12:25 Sr. Primary in class (40 min.), Jr. Primary in Singing Time (20 min.) & Sharing Time (20 min.)

12:25 - 12:30 Send Jr. Primary to class, bring in Sr. Primary for Sharing & Singing Time (5 min.)

12:30-1:10 Jr. Primary in class (40 min.) Sr. Primary in Singing Time (20 min.) Sharing Time (20 min.)

1:10 Dismiss for Sacrament Meeting

At precisely 11:45, I was to slip out to eat the small lunch I had brought with me—a tuna fish sandwich, a small bag of potato chips, a six-ounce can of apple juice, and a few celery sticks. I would have twenty minutes to eat during Singing Time. Then, when it was my turn to conduct Sharing Time, I would be available.

In reality, here's how our first Sunday in operation actually went:

11:15 In an attempt to hurry, I gave myself a *nasty* shot of insulin, which left a stinging bruise in my left hip.

11:40 Everyone was finally seated in the Primary room and we had secured their attention.

11:40 - 11:55 Opening Exercises. Natalie conducted. One of our two-minute inspirational talks took ten minutes as we agonized over every challenging word the eight-year-old read from *The Friend.*

11:55 - 12:25 Feeling a bit shaky, I slipped out to run a check on my blood sugar. Meanwhile, Natalie, Edna, and Gloria tried to herd the Sr. Primary to class and keep the Jr. Primary in the Primary room. I quickly discovered that I'd waited too long to eat, whipped out my sandwich, and wolfed it down. Too late I realized that I had selected to eat lunch in the classroom we'd assigned to the eleven Valiant boys, who angrily demanded to know why I was eating on Fast Sunday.

When my excuse of being a diabetic didn't wash, I gave them the celery sticks and beat a hasty retreat. Shortly afterwards, Natalie and I realized we'd forgotten to line up a substitute for these eleven-year-old boys who were now chasing each other down the hall throwing celery sticks. We sent Edna after them while I quickly finished my lunch in the girls' rest room.

Meanwhile, Gloria was doing her best to convince our somewhat temperamental chorister that she could still have the full twenty minutes she *desperately* needed for Singing Time, which would leave me approximately seven minutes for Sharing Time. I assured Natalie I didn't mind and gave the *Reader's Digest* condensed version of the Sharing Time I had spent all week preparing.

12:25 - 12:30 We played referee as the Sr. Primary stampeded over the Jr. Primary as they passed each other in the hallway, then tried to soothe several disgruntled Sr. Primary teachers whose class time had been cut short. When we promised things would be better next week, I wondered at our naivety.

12:30 - 1:10 Surprisingly, things went smoother during this second block of Primary. One eleven-year-old boy was missing, but Natalie felt confident she could find him. Still fighting my blood sugar, I stepped into the hall and reached into my purse for a candy bar, hoping to ward off a major reaction. I felt someone's eyes boring holes through me and looked down into the curious face of a four-year-old named Thomas Edwards, whose mother is my visiting teacher. He stared at the candy bar in my hand and sighed.

"Would you like some?" I asked, and he grinned. I broke off a small section of the Milky Way bar and gave it to him, then quickly devoured the rest of it. I looked up to see Thomas wiping the melted chocolate from his hand onto his freshly pressed white shirt. I quickly dragged him into the girls' rest room to clean off his shirt as best I could, ignoring his protests that only girls were allowed in this room. Snacks are forbidden in Primary—with the exception of the Nursery realm and lessons that call for such items. It was all in the Primary handbook. Fast Sundays were especially taboo. I could picture the outraged look on Patricia Edward's face and kept scrubbing until only a small unidentifiable brown stain was apparent.

As I discarded the wad of paper towels, I noticed that Thomas was fidgeting, holding himself in that endearing way small boys have. "Thomas, do you need to use the bathroom?" I asked. He nodded, informing me that was why he had originally come out into the hall. I pushed him toward one of the stalls, but he refused to cooperate, letting me know in no uncertain terms that he would not go potty in the girls' bathroom. I sighed and pulled Thomas from the room, guiding him toward the boys' rest room down the hall. By this time, he was in a bad way, but wasn't about to enter that room alone. I frantically glanced around, and seeing no one, I took a deep breath, grabbed Thomas, and rushed him into the rest room. Luckily, no one else seemed to be in the room, and Thomas quickly took care of his business. Just as we were about to leave, both of us feeling relieved, I heard a soft snicker. I followed a hunch and approached a metal stall. Peeking over the door, I found the missing eleven-year-old. I ordered him from the stall, gripped his arm tightly, and led both boys from the rest room, exiting just as Ed Bergen walked in, a questioning look on his red face. I forced a smile and continued on my way down the hall. Just then, a frustrated Natalie approached. I was five minutes late for my Sharing Time debut in the Sr. Primary. She had given up her search for the missing eleven-year-old to look for me. Edna had convinced her I had passed out somewhere in the church house. Shaking my head, I relinquished custody of the missing boy and Thomas to Natalie and hurried toward the Primary room, but not before I heard the four-year-old tell our Primary president that I was his potty friend.

1:10   We dismissed for Sacrament Meeting, our sanity questionable, but our testimonies intact.

Chapter 5

As Natalie had promised, the next Sunday was an improvement over the previous week's disaster. We were only five minutes late dismissing from Opening Exercises, and this time we had remembered to get a substitute for the eleven-year-old boys. Our most recent suggestion for a permanent teacher was still on hold; the man in question was out of town on vacation. I hoped this individual was having a wonderful time; these would be the last moments of peace he would enjoy for quite a while.

At the end of Primary, as the last cherubic face disappeared from the Primary room, Natalie told us we would soon have this new routine down pat. I questioned this, but didn't want to rain on her parade. But we *were* dealing with children. They were definitely a deciding factor in the great scheme of things.

By now, Thomas Edwards considered me his official potty friend. He refused to venture near the boys' rest room without me. Natalie saved me from continued embarrassment by convincing Brother Ed Bergen, the bishopric counselor over the Primary, to be on hand to escort Thomas into the tiled male domain each Sunday. A nervous Thomas made me promise I'd be waiting in the hall when he had finished. This arrangement worked out quite well for all of us.

Several of the children were worming their way into my life. There were times when something one of them did or said reminded me of Brook, but I was learning to push those memories aside, hoping that eventually the pain would soften.

Besides Thomas, there was an adorable little three-year-old

named Nancy Martin who lisped valiantly through every song Sister Gunderson struggled to teach the Jr. Primary. Then there were the Hale twins, Carrie and Sheri, two seven-year-olds who liked to live on the edge. Wende Hale, their mother, delighted in dressing the obnoxious tomboys in matching dresses, different colors, of course, to help us identify the identical twins. I knew the difference without the colorful dresses. Sheri was a born leader; Carrie, a devout follower. Sheri took pride in egging Carrie on, then she would sit back feigning innocence while her twin took the heat for whatever infraction had been committed. They were exasperating on occasion, but it was entertaining to see what they'd come up with next. I especially enjoyed the pranks they pulled on Sergeant Edna, as I called her under my breath. Edna's notebooks, pencils, and roll cards mysteriously moved from one location to another in the Primary room as our frustrated secretary began to believe that the youth of Zion were a lost cause.

I'll never forget the look on her face the Sunday her entire Primary bag of treasures disappeared. It was later found in the boys' rest room, which led me to believe the older boys were in on it. Regardless, it took a lot of coaxing from Natalie to convince Edna it was all in fun. That explanation failed to soothe a week later when a salt clay sculpture materialized on the small table Edna uses as a desk during Primary. With dark, twisted yarn glued to a wrinkled, rounded head and a fierce frown on its misshapen face, the sculpture bore an uncanny resemblance to our secretary. The Hale twins had created it in retaliation for the lecture they'd received from Edna the week before.

As I held the offending work of art in my hand, it took every ounce of self-discipline I could muster to keep a straight face when I spoke to Sheri and Carrie about the importance of showing respect to adults, which included *all* Primary leaders. Looking contrite, they muttered a quick apology to Edna, who continued to sulk. I volunteered to dispose of the statue and took it home to give it a place of honor on my computer desk.

But of all the children I looked forward to seeing each Sunday, one boy in particular captured a special place in my heart—shy, nine-year-old Hank Clawson.

Hank's parents had divorced when he was five. He lived in a small apartment with his inactive mother. We had been told to arrange rides for this young man who loved Primary and wanted to continue coming out to church. Mark and I had been picking him up the past couple of weeks. He rarely spoke, but his shy smile was thanks enough when we dropped him off in front of his apartment building after Sacrament Meeting each Sunday.

At the end of the month when Natalie said that someone else should take their turn with "Hank duty," I told her Mark and I would be only too happy to continue picking him up. It was right on our way, and we didn't have a large household to dress for church. Again Natalie gave me one of her stifling hugs, but I vowed to continue picking up Hank in spite of it.

As time passed, I became quite protective of Hank. I hated how the other kids picked on him. They made fun of his worn clothing and taunted him because he didn't fit in with their current standards of popular worthiness. My heart went out to this boy who wanted nothing more than to be accepted and loved. I made it a point to smile warmly whenever he glanced in my direction, and offered words of comfort and encouragement whenever the occasion presented itself.

Working in the Primary was an education. Not only was I learning to appreciate the distinct character traits each child possessed, but I was also learning to handle those unique situations that are a constant part of this organization—for example, coping with the continual overturn of teachers. As soon as we had a full operating staff, someone from another organization would steal our best teachers. I tended to be a bit indignant when this happened, but Natalie took it all in stride. Acting as though it was no big deal, she'd simply call for an emergency presidency meeting. As we tried to come up with replacements, I felt a lot like the little Dutch boy who had tried to plug the leaks in a dike with his fingers. Just as one hole was filled, another appeared out of nowhere! There were times when I thought it was hopeless, but somehow, we held it together.

I also decided there was a lot of truth in the expression that you're not a success unless you've upset someone. If this was the case, we were really doing well. When I shared that wisdom with Natalie, her eyes widened with concern. She wanted to know if we were causing contention in the ward. "Sure, Natalie," I said. "You can't believe the scandal we triggered by switching Sharing Time and Singing Time around." Natalie looked upset until I convinced her I was kidding.

I grew to hate Sunday morning phone calls. Usually it was a teacher with a pathetic excuse, begging for a reprieve from teaching that day. But I preferred those phone calls to the surprise no-shows. At least with a phone call, I had a few minutes warning and—most times—could arrange for a substitute. When a no-show occurred, it was a different story. On those occasions, if we couldn't nab someone at the last minute, we ended up filling in ourselves, struggling through lessons we had to wing—providing we could find an extra lesson manual. I quickly became adept at teaching off the top of my head or improvising with a game of chalkboard hangman, using Book of Mormon or Biblical characters or phrases.

Despite the challenges, as the weeks progressed, we gained new confidence in our positions. But, just when it looked like we had a handle on things, a rather startling transformation occurred. Natalie's two sons, nine-year-old Tyler and ten-year-old Jeremy had quickly become the terrors of Primary. Every time the unruly duo committed outrageous stunts, poor Natalie looked like she was going to have a stroke—much to the delight of the entire Sr. Primary. Natalie was usually forced to drag her two sons out into the hallway for a deserved tongue-lashing, but Jeremy and Tyler always came back grinning while Natalie returned looking like a casualty of war.

After one unfortunate episode that had involved gum and the long blonde tresses of an eleven-year-old girl, Natalie nearly came unglued. She breathed deeply, her face a brilliant shade of red, her eyes sending a clear message: *Someone else handle this or I'm going to kill these two!* Luckily, Ed Bergen happened to be visiting the Primary that day, and he escorted the two culprits out into the hall for a stern lecture. Gloria and Edna hurried the wailing victim of the prank into the kitchen down the hall, and Sister Gunderson began a rousing chorus of "Nephi's Courage," with the rest of the Sr. Primary while I guided Natalie down to the girls' rest room. I grabbed a handful of tissue from a nearby stall and handed it to her.

"I'm sorry, Teri. I don't normally lose it like this, but, I don't know what to do with those two monsters anymore."

"Oh, I'm sure they're just—"

"They're rotten! And it's all my fault!"

I was shocked at her intensity. "Natalie, that's not true," I said in the most comforting tone I could muster.

She shook her head almost violently. "No, it's my fault. Jerry says I'm too lenient with them. That if I'd take a firmer stance at home . . ." Her wavering voice faltered and she turned away to dab at her eyes.

I tapped my fingers on the counter and wondered where the father in question was. "Maybe Jerry should talk to the boys—"

Natalie whirled around to face me. For the first time, I saw a trace of fear in those beautiful blue eyes. "No. It's okay. I'll handle this. It's my responsibility."

"Natalie, they're his kids too. Maybe if he knew—"

"No, Teri," she said, her voice high and strained. "Jerry's out of town this weekend on a business trip. The last thing he'll want to hear when he gets home tomorrow is how his sons acted up in Primary."

I frowned, certain she wasn't telling me everything. "Natalie— "

Uncharacteristically, she cut me off again. "It's okay. I'm fine. It's just been one of those days."

"You're sure?" I asked.

The panic in her eyes had changed to grim determination. "Positive," she said firmly. "Now, let's get back to Primary." All signs of emotional strain had disappeared as Natalie slipped back into the familiar role of Mrs. Perfection. Once I had believed it; now I wondered if it was just an act.

Chapter 6

Halfway through November, we were faced with our first quarterly Primary activity. In our ward, it was a time-honored custom that the week before Christmas, the Primary organization would put on an old-fashioned Christmas pageant, complete with the traditional nativity scene. After the closing prayer, Santa would make an appearance, bearing gifts for the children in the ward. When faced with the magnitude of this impending ordeal, I was ready to jump ship. As the first counselor, it was my responsibility to direct such productions. When Natalie shared this with me, I demanded to see the contract I had somehow been coerced into signing for this calling.

"I must have missed that part of my Primary contract," I argued, "Natalie, no one said anything about this before."

Before Natalie could speak, I said quickly, "Oh, I get it. I must have missed the fine print."

Natalie grinned and said easily, "It will be a breeze. With your creativity, you're a natural. This will be the best Christmas Pageant this ward's ever seen!"

She was referring to the fact that I write daily columns for the *Post Register*, the local newspaper. Everyone assumes that because I handle the Community News section, I'm a natural in the creativity department. I'd run into this false assumption before.

"I report on society events that take place in Idaho Falls. I'd hardly call it being creative."

"But your columns always have such flair. Such style."

"I've never written a play in my life. I can't even write a roadshow. Remember *Dallas in Blunderland?*"

Natalie was suddenly silent but her obvious wince told me she remembered vividly the major humiliation our ward had suffered three years ago. "That was you?" she asked quietly. Her enthusiasm quickly waned.

I nodded. Taking a seat beside her on the couch, I said, "I'm not that gifted. I have limitations. There's no way—"

"I have an idea," Gloria said suddenly. Natalie and I both stared across the Cox living room at her. "What if we did a scene from Santa's workshop? You know, have some of the kids dress up like toy soldiers, dolls, and jack-in-the-boxes."

"That would be cute," Natalie replied enthusiastically and grinned at me. "See what a little team effort can do? We'll work on this together. With Gloria's ideas and your talent for writing, it'll be great!"

I was trapped. I could sense it. It was as obvious as the grin on Natalie's face. Sighing, I stared dismally at the spotless carpet. The doorbell rang and Natalie jumped to her feet to answer the door. Edna's booming voice echoed throughout the house.

"Sorry I'm late. I was heading out the door when the phone rang. It was my boy, Ed. That son of mine can't go a week without checking in." She entered the living room, beaming with pleasure.

"That's okay, Edna," Natalie said, taking Edna's coat from her. Since Natalie had commented that Edna usually arrived fifteen to twenty minutes early for our presidency meetings, we were a little surprised when she hadn't shown up this morning. I had been feeling relieved myself, a feeling that quickly left as her piercing gaze fixed on me.

"Teri, you're awfully pale today. Are you feeling all right?"

Here we go again, I thought, shaking my head.

She misinterpreted the shake of my head."I knew it," she barked, "Natalie, go get that girl some juice!"

I gave Natalie a look that said, *You come in here with a glass of juice and you'll be wearing it!*

"Edna, she's fine," Natalie reassured her. "We're all a little concerned about the Christmas Pageant, but—listen to this. Gloria had a wonderful idea." She neatly distracted Edna and won my undying gratitude.

An hour later, we had nearly outlined the envisioned play. As we wrapped up our brainstorming session, the phone rang. Natalie walked into the kitchen to answer. Edna took advantage of the lull in the meeting to impart some of her wisdom on the fine art of pregnancy to Gloria. *Now's a good time to check the old blood sugar,* I decided. Picking up my purse, I headed down the hall to the large bathroom. A quick test confirmed that I was running low, so I pulled a small can of apple juice from my purse and drained the contents. I discarded the empty can in the peach-colored garbage container, covering it with a handful of unused tissue paper to hide it. To add credence to my disappearance, I reached for the small handle and flushed. I even went so far as to run water in the sink for a couple of minutes to avoid a hygiene lecture from Sergeant Edna. Pleased with my artful deception, I started back to the living room. Then I heard Natalie's voice.

"I'm sorry, Jerry. It won't happen again—I promise!"

I turned around, wanting to stay out of what appeared to be a typical husband-wife disagreement. Jerry must have telephoned from work, and Natalie had moved from the kitchen phone to the one in the master bedroom for privacy.

"Jerry . . . please, honey, let's talk about it later. I'm right in the middle of a presidency meeting . . . Jerry, you don't understand—"

Concern, and a reporter's sense that something was up, rooted me in place.

"Please don't say that! You don't mean it." Her voice trembled as if she were near tears. "Jerry . . . I'm doing the best I—"

It was silent, except for a muffled sob. "We'll talk about it later." I heard a soft click as she hung up the phone. I hurried as quietly as I could down the hall toward the living room.

"You all right?" Edna queried with her usual tact.

I nodded and asked Gloria how she thought we should work in the nativity scene at the end of the pageant. She listed several ideas, but I was only half listening as I kept an eye on the hall. A few minutes later, Natalie appeared, looking as radiant as ever. Had I imagined the pain and stress in her voice? Perplexed, I doodled all over my notebook as the conversation went on without me. Something was wrong here, I was sure of it.

"Well, that should take care of it. Right, Teri?"

I glanced up at Natalie. "Right."

"And you're okay with Gloria's suggestion for the ending?"

I was in trouble. "Uh, which suggestion are we talking about?"

Natalie lifted an eyebrow and gave me a funny look. "The one you agreed to not more than two minutes ago."

"Oh. That one," I replied, totally lost. "Could you run it by me again?" I asked.

"Teri, have you checked your blood sugar lately?" Edna demanded. For the first time I was grateful to Edna for giving me a way out. It wouldn't be hard to fake the role of the confused diabetic on the verge of a reaction. "I . . . uh . . . what were you saying . . . uh, Gloria? I mean, Natalie." I held out one hand and improvised the shaking that sometimes goes with a reaction.

"Well, would you look at that. This girl is in trouble. I knew it! I said to myself, I said, 'Edna, that girl is much too quiet.' Natalie, go get a glass of juice!"

Rising, Natalie studied my face, looking for the warning she usually found there.

"It's okay," I stammered. "Juice might be a good idea."

Natalie hurried from the room, returning shortly with a glass of orange juice. She handed me the glass and sat directly in front of me on the coffee table. Edna had already flown to my side to check my pulse. It was a good thing I was nervous; my pulse rate was up a bit. Edna seemed pleased.

"Drink the juice, Teri, that heart of yours is racing. She's in a reaction," Edna added, smiling brightly at the other two. "I've seen this before. She'll be all right," she said with authority, patting Natalie's knee. "Don't you worry. I'll pull her through this."

It was tempting to blow a mouthful of orange juice at Edna. I gritted my teeth and swallowed it down like a good patient.

Later, after checking my blood sugar to make sure it was normal, I drove home. The women had not been easily convinced that I was capable of functioning as a driver, and they had all offered to drive me home. Needless to say, once I had finally pulled out of Natalie's driveway, I cranked the radio the max. But the music once again refused to absorb my frustration. Defeated, I turned off the radio and reflected on everything I knew about Jerry Cox.

A successful insurance agent, Jerry was handsome and clean cut. In fact, I had sometimes wondered if he was a little on the vain side, considering the care he took with his appearance. Every jet-black hair of his head was always carefully groomed into place. His shoes were so shiny you could see your reflection in them, and his tailored shirts were ironed to perfection. I was sure Natalie had something to do with the latter offense, giving me further cause to resent the woman. At times Mark would glance at Jerry, then down at his own semi-wrinkled shirts, gaze in my direction, and sigh.

Ironing is not one of my talents. Mark knew this when he married me. During our courtship era at BYU, he had made the mistake one afternoon of bringing over a wrinkled white shirt he needed for the next day. Anxious to show off my limited domestic capabilities, I had borrowed my roommate's iron to attack the offending wrinkles. I had just started when the phone rang. Naturally, it was for me. As I balanced the phone against one ear with my shoulder and continued ironing, demonstrating my ability to accomplish several things at the same time, I didn't notice I was leaving the iron in place longer than was necessary. To this day, Mark bemoans the fate of his favorite good-luck white shirt from his mission. After the demise of this much loved possession, I refused to iron any of Mark's clothes. To keep peace in the family, we're into permanent press. We tend to ignore the few wrinkles that still manage to surface.

Mark's mother gave us an iron for our first anniversary. I smiled and added it to the collection we had received at our reception. When he's really desperate, Mark gets one out once in a while. As for myself, I make sure Mark isn't around when I break out the iron. I'd hate for him to learn I've become quite efficient in this area of domestic drudgery.

As I continued to compare Jerry with Mark and some of the other men in our ward, it was obvious there were glaring differences. The longer I thought about it, the more it seemed that Jerry was always a little too perfect, a little too well dressed. At the annual Elders Basketball Tournament in our stake, Jerry had stood out from the other players with his two-piece warm-up suit, black with purple stripes. He even wore a matching headband. The other men all wore sweats, shorts, and T-shirts in varying degrees of disarray. Most didn't even match, which supported my personal theory that men are color-blind.

Jerry was obviously an exception to the rule. Slipping out of his expensive warm-up suit, he walked onto the court in his black shorts and purple tanktop. In contrast, Mark wore a ragged T-shirt and an old pair of sweats.

During the game, which was supposed to be an opportunity to fellowship the less active members, Jerry had taken to heart a bad call made by one of the refs. He all but threw himself over the foul that had been called, and had nearly been awarded a technical to go with it. The Elders Quorum president had pulled Jerry from the game and replaced him with Mark. While Jerry fumed on the bench, his teammates fumbled with the basketball, often losing it to the other team. By the end of the game, the other team had won, and Jerry stormed from the gym, refusing to speak to his fellow ward members or congratulate the opposing team.

Dude with an attitude, I'd thought. On the way home, Mark mused that Jerry had taken the fun out of the game by being so competitive, and added, "I can't believe what a perfectionist he's become."

Now, on the way home from presidency meeting I pondered Mark's comments as I gripped the steering wheel. Was Jerry as demanding with Natalie as he had been with his teammates? At the time, I had chalked his behavior up to the aggressiveness that often goes along with sports. But was there more to it than that? Feeling troubled, I pulled into the garage, anxious to pump my husband for more information. He'd gone to high school with Jerry. Maybe he could shed some light on the situation. I knew he'd probably say my imagination was getting the best of me. What I'd heard was very likely a disagreement between a husband and wife. I hoped that was the case.

Chapter 7

"And?" Mark asked as he loosened his tie. He had just returned home from the computer store he manages, a quaint little shop known as the Software House.

"And that was all I heard," I said, realizing how silly this must sound. "Look, Mark, it wasn't so much what she said, but how she said it. It was obvious the woman was at the end of her rope."

"Of course, you yourself have never felt that way with me," he teased, his brown eyes twinkling. He had anchored his tie around his thick head of brown hair and apparently thought he looked quite dashing.

"Okay, maybe they were both having a bad day. It happens. There are occasions when I could cheerfully smack you upside your head, like now for instance," I commented, reaching for a sofa pillow. Within minutes, we were having a serious pillow fight. After recovering from a hard blow to the head, I regained my bearings and returned a major swipe to Mark's stomach, effectively knocking the wind out of him. Just then, the doorbell rang.

"You get it," Mark puffed, trying to catch his breath. I nodded and hurried to answer, still clutching my chosen weapon. As I approached the door, I realized how my hair must look. It was too late to do anything about it now. I tried to smooth the wild hair back into place and courageously opened the door. Natalie's eyes seemed to take in my hair, the pillow in my hand, and my rumpled appearance, her face stricken. I followed her gaze and saw that two of my buttons had come undone. I'm not sure which one of us blushed more.

Mark didn't help matters. With his tie still attached to his head, he stumbled into the entry way behind me, looking as disheveled as I was. Wheezing, he stopped short to stare at Natalie.

Natalie quickly focused on the cement porch. "I . . . seem to have come at a bad time," she stammered, turning to go. "I should've called first. Sorry."

"No, Natalie, wait," I pleaded, handing Mark my pillow. I hurriedly rebuttoned my blouse. "This isn't what you think." I could feel the blush creep back into my face. "We were having a little pillow fight, that's all."

Natalie stared at us curiously as I tried to explain. "Mark was being obnoxious. I was putting him in his place."

"She throws a hefty punch," Mark added, as he slipped his tie back around his neck. "She had just knocked the wind out of me when the doorbell rang. A lucky break for her."

Still looking uncomfortable, Natalie refused to step closer. I flipped the porch light on and saw that she had been crying. "What's wrong, Natalie?" I asked.

"Nothing's wrong," she said brightly. "I just wanted to make sure you were all right. I was worried after the reaction earlier. I'll call you tomorrow." She turned to leave.

"Natalie, it's fine, really. Come in," I insisted, convinced something was up. I ran down the steps and dragged her back up the porch. Mark moved out of the way, giving me a curious look as I led Natalie into the house. I showed her to the room that serves as my office at home, flipped on the light, and closed the door. "Have a seat," I pointed to the swivel chair near my computer desk.

She remained standing. "I shouldn't have come," she said, staring down at her hands. "Jerry will be worried. I've been driving around for a couple of hours. I don't know why I pulled up in your driveway. I never even thought that you and Mark . . . that is . . . I never meant to intrude." She stammered to a halt.

I gently pushed her down into the swivel chair, then sat next to her in a plastic chair. "Natalie, I promise you didn't interrupt anything. Honest, we were just having a pillow fight."

"Really?" she asked shyly, the blush slowly fading from her face.

In the bright light of the room, I noticed that a portion of her face was still red, but at the time I shrugged it off as the result of her continued embarrassment. "Scout's honor," I promised, holding up two fingers. "Mark was being a smart aleck, so I hit him with a sofa pillow. Next thing I know, we were having a full-blown, knock-down, drag-out war." I smiled and hoped the explanation would ease the tension in the room, but the look on Natalie's face told me I hadn't quite succeeded.

I tried again. "Mark and I have a lot of pillow fights. It's a good way to get rid of stress. I'll admit, things got a little wild tonight. He'd managed to knock me across the living room before the doorbell rang, which explains my latest hairstyle," I quipped, patting my uncooperative hair. "I had no idea my shirt had come unbuttoned. I could've died when I looked down and saw I was suffering from 'gapitous'." I laughed nervously, hoping Natalie would join me. She didn't.

"Sometimes I envy you and Mark," she said quietly, not meeting my eyes.

"Natalie . . ." I began, then realized that I didn't know what to say.

"You have so much fun together. And Mark always seems so supportive." A single tear wandered down the side of her face.

"What is it?" I asked.

"I'm feeling sorry for myself. Jerry came home early from work. We had an argument and I stormed out. It's nothing . . . really."

I didn't believe her. "Then why are you still crying?" That was certainly the wrong thing to say! She immediately erupted in a fountain of tears, and I dashed around the room, frantically searching for a box of tissue. Then I remembered I'd emptied it last week during a brief encounter with a vicious cold. I left the room and hurried down the hall to the bathroom for fresh supplies. On the way back, Mark stopped me.

"Is she all right?" he asked with a concerned frown.

I shook my head, fingering the box of Kleenex in my hands.

"Keep me posted," he whispered. I nodded and moved back to the study.

Natalie's emotional downpour lasted for nearly twenty minutes. Then, as quickly as it had started, it was over. I'd spent the time offering tissues and comfort as best I knew how. Finally handing her the box of Kleenex, I moved toward the east window and waited to give her time to compose herself. The window looked out on our small flower bed, which I take pride in during the spring and summer months. Now the earthy bed was frosted over with a thin layer of snow. I envisioned the snowman I'd like to construct in the near future, weather permitting. At the moment, there wasn't enough snow around for even a proper snowball fight.

I'd had several of those with Mark during the past seven winters. I smiled, remembering last year's stunning victory. I'd hit my husband with so many snowballs in a row he'd begged for mercy. It was then that the real battle had begun. As I'd moved to his side to offer sympathy, he had gripped me in a fierce bear hug, plunging me into a snowbank where he proceeded to wash my face in the snow. Later, he'd kissed away each flake. Enjoying the memory, I reflected on how wonderful my husband was—most of the time.

The sound of Natalie vigorously blowing her nose brought me back to the crisis at hand. I turned from the window and offered what I hoped was a compassionate smile.

"You must think I'm a total nut case," she said, wiping at her eyes with a fresh tissue.

I shook my head, amazed by how attractive Natalie still looked despite her reddened, puffy eyes. One cheek was slightly swollen, but again, I dismissed it as merely evidence of her recent crying episode. When I give in to a good cry, I usually resemble someone with a massive crop of hives. Not Natalie. She looked like one of those tragic heroines from the silver screen. Sighing, I crossed the room and sat beside her. "Want to talk about it?"

"I'm not sure." She dabbed at her eyes again. Afraid that I would say the wrong thing, I remained silent, hesitantly patting her shoulder. She rose to her feet and moved to the window. "I appreciate everything you've done tonight, Teri," she started. I protested, certain I had only managed to make a fool of myself and offer Kleenex.

Her somber look silenced me and she continued, "I've never been very close to the women in our ward. They've always seemed a little distant. It's probably silly, but I get the impression that for some reason, they resent me." I shifted uncomfortably in my chair. "This is the first time I've really felt I belonged since we moved here five years ago. I feel like you three are my only friends."

I continued to sit in silence, unsure of what to say. I liked Natalie, but I'd never thought of her as a friend.

"Jerry can be so critical sometimes," Natalie continued softly. "And since I was put in as Primary president, it's gotten worse. He says it's taking up too much of my time—time that should be spent doing things for the family. But honestly, if I didn't have this calling I think I'd go crazy. It's the only break I have from my family." She paused and gave me an embarrassed look. "I didn't mean that the way it sounded. I love Jerry and the kids. But, sometimes, I need time for me.

"Only Jerry doesn't see it that way." She stared out the window and sighed. "I don't know why he's acting like this. He wasn't always so . . ." she hesitated, searching for the right word. I thought of one for her, though I doubted she would agree. "He's always been so thoughtful and kind," Natalie continued. "Then, two years ago, his father had a heart attack. His death did something to Jerry. You see, Jerry and his father weren't on very good terms, although I'd always hoped they would work things out. Now it's too late." The words rushed out, as if a pressure gauge had been released. Shocked by what I was hearing, I quietly listened as the woman I had wrongly dubbed "Mrs. Perfection" poured her heart out.

Later that evening, I drove Natalie home. We left in my Prism, with Mark and Bishop Anderson following in Natalie's car. Natalie had begged us to let her drive home alone, but none of us felt it was a good idea.

After Natalie and I had finally made an appearance from the study, we found that Mark had followed a hunch and called Bishop Anderson. The bishop had hurried over and spent nearly an hour counseling Natalie in our study while Mark and I waited in the living room.

When Bishop Anderson guided Natalie back to the living room, he asked Mark to assist him in giving her a blessing. A calming spirit of peace and love filled the room as the bishop blessed her with the courage and strength to get through this crisis. Afterwards, we tried to come up with a workable plan of action. The bishop felt strongly that the three of us needed to escort Natalie home. He reminded her of the promise made during the blessing that all would be well, gave us an encouraging smile, and suggested we begin the short journey to the Cox residence.

My mind was in a whirl as I slid behind the wheel of my car. It still filled me with rage every time I thought about Jerry striking Natalie. According to Natalie, he had never laid a hand on her, until earlier tonight. Tonight he had snapped over something so trivial—two little wrinkles in his shirt—that it was obvious he was out of control. That was what he had called to discuss with her during our Presidency meeting. He'd even come home early from work to talk with her about it. At home after our meeting, she had told him that he was making something out of nothing and he had slapped her. That was when she had left the house, driving around in a daze until pulling into our driveway.

Now, as we turned down the street that led to her home, I knew she was afraid this would set Jerry off again.

"I should've come alone. He's not going to like this."

"Natalie—"

"He's a good man, Teri," she said so softly, I almost thought I'd imagined it. "He was upset today."

"He was wrong to hit you."

"I don't think he meant to," she spoke hesitantly.

"Maybe not," I said, "But still—"

"I'm sure this happens between lots of couples," she said hopefully. "Look at you and Mark tonight. You said he knocked you across the living room."

"Natalie, there's a big difference here. Mark and I were playing around. Besides, you can't compare pillows to fists. What Jerry did was wrong! And it's more than the slap he gave you tonight."

Natalie gazed in the darkness at me.

"I noticed the way you panicked over how your boys were acting in Primary a couple of weeks ago. I thought you were going to have the fantods when I mentioned Jerry ought to be told about it. Then earlier today, the phone call that came during our meeting. I was in the bathroom. When I came out, I heard you. I didn't mean to eavesdrop but—"

"You heard what I said to Jerry?"

"Part of it," I admitted as I pulled up along the curb in front of her house.

"So you know I hung up on him. It was my fault. I should've handled things differently. Then none of this—"

"You didn't do anything wrong," I said firmly. I killed the engine and turned to look at her. "Didn't any of that blessing sink in tonight? You don't deserve to be treated like this. No one does. And if things don't go well now with the bishop and Jerry, you and your kids are more than welcome to stay with us for as long as you need to."

"Thanks," she said in a choked voice. "I feel so ashamed. If any of this gets out in the ward or community . . ."

I slipped an arm around her trembling shoulders and gave her an intense squeeze. "I'm the one who should feel ashamed. Remember how silly I looked earlier?" I said in a poor attempt to cheer her up.

She smiled. "I don't think I'll ever forget the look on your face when you answered the door. Then I could've died thinking . . ." she couldn't quite say it but I knew what she meant.

"Enough said," I said quickly. "I get the idea. Now, just so we understand each other, everything you've said tonight will remain between us, just as the little pillow fight Mark and I had earlier will also remain a secret, right?"

"Right."

"Good girl. We need to keep these things quiet. Imagine the lectures we would get from Sergeant Edna." As we pictured the woman's stern face, we both started to laugh. It was a wonderful release. We were still laughing when we got out of the car, much to the astonishment of the bishop and Mark.

We made our way to the front door of Natalie's house, then stepped aside letting Bishop Anderson go in first, as we had previously decided. The rest of us followed, hoping the bishop's presence would defuse any remaining anger on Jerry's part. We needn't have worried. Jerry, looking as haggard and unkempt as I've ever seen him, practically knocked us down to reach Natalie's side.

"Natalie, honey, I'm so sorry. I don't know what got into me. I'd never hurt you . . . I didn't mean . . . it'll never happen again, I promise." His anguished eyes searched hers for forgiveness. Natalie fell into his arms with a sob. As they shared what should've been an intimate moment, Mark and I studied the carpet, while the bishop examined his fingernails. Finally remembering he had an audience, Jerry drew back from Natalie but wouldn't look directly at any of us. Bishop Anderson crossed the room to shake his hand.

"Is there somewhere we can talk?" he asked.

Hesitantly nodding, Jerry glanced at Mark. Mark forced a smile, moved across the room and as a gesture of friendship, shook Jerry's hand. Then Jerry led the bishop into a room down the hall.

At this point, the Cox children moved into view. Natalie's five-year-old daughter ran into the living room to give her mommy a hug. Looking quite somber, her two sons approached. I exchanged an uncomfortable glance with Mark, then hit upon an idea. "Have you kids eaten supper yet?"

All three shook their heads.

"We had some cookies and Lifesavers," Tyler volunteered.

"I'm still hungry," Kimberly commented as she pulled on her mother's hand.

"Say, guys, my husband, Mark," I said, gesturing to my husband, "has been known to make a peanut butter and jelly sandwich that is out of this world. Why don't you show him where things are in the kitchen and I'll stay in here to keep your mommy company."

Mark quirked his eyebrows at me, but Natalie's children appeared relieved to have someone take charge of their lives again. They chirped with excitement as they led my husband out of the living room.

Natalie sank onto the couch, looking as exhausted as I felt. "Thanks, Teri. I'm really not up to much right now. And the last thing those kids need to see is me breaking down again."

I nodded and sat beside her. Figuring this might take a while, I unzipped my coat, wiggled out of it, and placed it on the arm of the sofa.

"I'm almost positive that's why Jeremy and Tyler have been such a handful lately. They're old enough to know things have been tense between Jerry and me."

I helped Natalie out of her coat, quietly listening as she described the various worries and sources of stress in her life. It was obvious that she really needed to unload; she'd kept things inside that would've destroyed a weaker person. My admiration for her continued to grow as the evening progressed. *Natalie is a real person*, I thought. *With problems and frustrations just like the rest of us.* It did my heart good to know I wasn't the only one who questioned the fairness of life.

"You know, Nat," I said (Natalie seemed much too formal after what we'd been through), "I've got a theory like that myself. I think I signed a contract in the pre-existence, but it was rushed by me so fast I didn't get a chance to read the fine print. You know, there are some things in my life *I know* I never would have agreed to."

Natalie smiled "You said something like that earlier today—at our meeting," she gently reminded me.

"What?" I was astonished. "Was that today? It seems like last week."

"Last year, you mean," she added as she kicked off her shoes. Settling back against the couch, she rested her feet on the coffee table. As she wiggled her toes, I looked on with envy. "Go ahead," she encouraged. "Take off your shoes and kick back."

I grinned at the invitation, quickly removed my pumps, and propped my feet on the table beside hers. Mark poked his head around the corner, stared for a minute, then focused on Natalie.

"Your children are through eating. What should—"

Natalie sat up and looked at her watch. "Oh, no! It's ten after eleven. I forgot how late it was. The kids have school tomorrow—"

I put a hand on her arm. "Natalie, it's Saturday tomorrow. They'll be fine. Let them sleep in."

"Oh. That's right. But, what if . . . ?" she glanced fearfully down the hall.

I met her worried expression with what I hoped was a calm demeanor. "I really think things are going to work out. I was worried earlier, but now that we're here, I feel like it's going to be okay."

Mark smiled and nodded in agreement. "I felt that same prompting during the blessing the bishop gave you."

"See, we even have Mark's word on the matter," I said brightly. "Things'll turn out. Now, you just sit here and relax while I help Mark put the kids to bed." I slipped my shoes on and followed my husband out of the living room. He agreed to tuck in Jeremy and Tyler while I looked after Kimberly's bedtime needs, which included two drinks of water and a lengthy bedtime story. Twenty minutes later, Mark and I rendezvoused back in the living room. As we rounded the corner, I raised a finger to my lips. Natalie had fallen asleep on the couch. We retreated back down the hall and I went to find an extra blanket.

I had just covered Natalie with it when the bishop and a shaken Jerry emerged from the guest room. Jerry's eyes looked as swollen and red as Natalie's had been. He gazed at Mark, then me, then at his sleeping wife.

"Is she all right?" he stammered.

"She's had a rough night," I answered, trying to keep a handle on the anger I still felt toward Jerry. He had caused Natalie an untold amount of pain. In my opinion, he deserved to suffer.

"I . . . I am sorry." He looked again at Mark. "Mark, you've known me for a long time . . . You know I've never acted like this . . ."

"No, you haven't," Mark replied. "But I think we both remember someone else who did."

I raised an eyebrow and stared at my husband. What was Mark saying?

Bishop Anderson lifted a hand as if to ward off any negative discussion. "There's no need to rehash the past." He smiled kindly and put an arm around Jerry's slumped shoulders.

Jerry met my disapproving stare with an expression of misery and pain. Despite my misgivings, I could see he regretted what had taken place. We were so preoccupied, none of us noticed that Natalie had awakened from her nap on the couch. She quietly approached her husband, glancing first at the bishop, then at Jerry.

"Natalie . . . can you ever forgive me?" Jerry stammered.

Tears came to Natalie's eyes as she nodded. Jerry hesitated, then took her in his arms. Nodding his approval, Bishop Anderson indicated we should leave. I retrieved my coat from the couch while Mark moved into the kitchen to find his. Together we walked out into the night air. We'd caught on that the bishop wanted some time alone with the couple. As we waited in the car, I questioned Mark about what he'd said earlier.

"What did you mean when you said you remembered someone else who acted like Jerry did tonight?"

"Jerry's dad. He was a big guy . . . used to be a Marine. He thought the best way to keep his family in line was through strict rules and corporal punishment."

"You mean Jerry's dad . . ." I paused, unable to finish the sentence.

Mark nodded. "I hated spending the night at Jerry's house when we were growing up," Mark continued. "My parents weren't too thrilled about it either. Jerry's dad had a reputation for drinking. So most of the time, we stayed at my place, or our friend Pete's. There was always so much yelling and fighting going on with Jerry's family. I never saw any of the physical stuff, but Jerry told me his dad slapped his mother around at times. Jerry hated his dad for it. He hated how his father expected them to be perfect. It makes it hard to understand why Jerry would start acting just like his dad."

I thought a moment. "Natalie mentioned Jerry's father passed away a couple of years ago. She said that was when the trouble began."

"And you're sure tonight was the first time he's ever hit her?"

"Pretty sure. Once she started opening up, Natalie laid all of the cards on the table. She said Jerry's yelled a lot, mostly over silly things, but has never hurt her physically until tonight."

I glanced at the house; the bishop was walking toward the car. I quickly opened the door on my side, slipped out, and climbed into the back.

"I can sit back there," Bishop Anderson chided. "But first, Mark, would you assist me in giving Jerry a blessing? I'd thought about it earlier, but wasn't going to push the issue, hoping he'd bring it up. He finally did, and I'd like you to help me."

"Sure," Mark answered, climbing out of the car.

The bishop looked at me. "Natalie asked that you come back in for this." I nodded and followed the two men to the house.

Natalie seemed happier after her husband's blessing. Jerry still looked haggard, but his eyes showed a look of determination that hadn't been there before. Mark and Bishop Anderson shook hands with Jerry while I gave Natalie a hug. After another round of good-byes, we left the house a second time. I opened the door on my side of the car and quickly moved into the back seat.

"Young lady," Bishop Anderson said with a grin, "I meant what I said earlier. You don't have to ride back there."

I smiled back at him. "But this way, you won't have to climb over me to get out."

"I guess you have a point. Thanks."

On the way home, the bishop asked us to keep in touch with Natalie and Jerry. "And keep a lid on this, will you? Teri, you've been a good friend to Sister Cox," he said. "I can see why she was inspired to choose you as a counselor."

I felt a twinge of guilt. I hadn't been *that* good of a friend to Natalie. At least, not yet. Silently, I vowed things would change, hoping Sally would understand. No one would ever replace her, but right now Natalie needed a friend.

Chapter 8

During the weeks that followed, Jerry and Natalie saw a Church-approved counselor recommended by Bishop Anderson. In the meantime, I was to keep the Primary on course so Natalie would have time to work things out with her husband. Within two weeks, however, she proved she could handle the situation at home and Primary with an ease that was astounding. Natalie and Jerry went somewhere together that first weekend, and by the following week, the bruise on her face had disappeared. As things improved at home, the Cox boys behaved accordingly. They still had their moments, but they usually managed to act as well as the other boys in our ward.

As a courtesy to Natalie, and to relieve some of the pressure, I suggested to Edna and Gloria that we take turns playing hostess for our biweekly meetings. We held the next meeting at my humble abode. Edna showed up twenty minutes early, but I was prepared. Heeding Natalie's warning, I had timed it so that all last-minute tidying up was finished five minutes before Edna was due to arrive.

I think the woman was a bit disappointed. She wandered around the house, hoping to find something undone or out of place. Housework isn't my idea of fun, but I had taken great pains to look impressive for her and gleaned a certain satisfaction from the defeated look on her face when she couldn't find anything to complain about. She sighed heavily, removed her coat, and handed it to me to hang up. Almost gloating, I moved toward the coat closet and opened the door, forgetting I'd stashed various odds and ends inside at the last minute. The opened door triggered an avalanche of tremendous proportions, and I was buried in a pile of games, puzzles, hats, gloves, and vacuum cleaner attachments. I moaned pitifully as Edna gleefully dug me out, clucking with obvious delight.

I spent the next fifteen minutes reorganizing the entire closet, under the close supervision of Sergeant Edna. When Natalie arrived, she helped me restack a pile of games while Edna continued to expound on the evils of clutter. By the time Gloria arrived, we had finally passed closet inspection. As Edna happily filled Gloria in on the sordid details of my grievous sin, Gloria stifled a smile and nodded a hello in my direction.

"I'm sorry I'm late," she said apologetically. The reason, we learned, was that her tumultuous stomach hadn't cooperated this morning. But now she was feeling better and was eager to get to work on the script for our upcoming Christmas production.

The past week I had attempted to pull a rough draft together. It was in the archives of my word processor, buried in the depths of my computer. As I led everyone down the hall toward the study, I was puzzled by the worried look on Natalie's face. She leaned forward and whispered her concern to me. I gasped. I'd completely forgotten all about the Sergeant Edna doll still sitting on my computer desk. I was certain of impending doom, but Natalie came to my rescue. She stepped back. "Edna," she said, trying to sound anxious, "my daughter has developed a rash and I wonder . . ."

Hurrying into the study, I quickly grabbed the offending doll and shoved it under a pile of papers in a drawer, closing it as Gloria walked in.

"So, this is where you get your creative juices flowing," she commented, gazing around at the room. "Is that an IBM or a Macintosh?" she asked, moving to my computer.

"Actually, it's an IBM-compatible."

"Three-eighty-six?"

"Four-eighty-six with a double-speed CD-ROM drive," I answered, surprised at her interest.

"Wow. Is the CD-ROM really worth the extra money?"

I had to laugh. "My husband thinks so."

"Does he use the computer a lot?" Gloria sounded more than a little envious.

I smiled as I thought about Mark. He was in the height of his glory surrounded by computers. It was understandable that he wanted the top of the line in his own home. Next to me, it was his great joy in life. "He likes the games," I finally replied. "And the graphics on a CD-ROM are unsurpassed," I added, imitating my husband.

Gloria laughed and ran her fingers over the keyboard. "I worked as a computer processor before Ian and I got married," she said wistfully. "I'd planned on working for at least a couple of years. But now, with the baby coming . . ." she paused and I could see that tears were about to form. What was this, Crisis Month in the Fourth Ward?

Pushing the button that brought the computer to life, I offered Gloria the driver's seat and let her amuse herself browsing through the software stored on the hard drive. About five minutes later, Natalie entered the room and gave me a look that said, *You owe me big time!* Edna was hot on her heels, continuing with her lecture on the outbreak of rashes and the necessary treatments for said discomforts. I stifled a grin and guided Gloria into my word processor files, helping her access the document I had labeled: PagntDis.

"PagntDis?" Gloria asked.

"Yeah, it's the pet name I've given this production," I said with a grin.

Natalie gazed thoughtfully in my direction. "Let me guess, Pageant Disaster?" she said. It was astounding how well our president could read me these days. I nodded and quickly retrieved the offending document.

"Now, Teri," Edna started, the tone of her voice indicating I was in for a lecture. Natalie gave me a look that implied it served me right. "We have to think positively," Edna continued. "Negative thoughts clutter our minds and it's a proven fact negative thoughts can affect a person's health. Why I remember a seminar where we learned . . ."

Politely ignoring most of what the retired nurse was saying, I gestured for Gloria to scroll through the rough draft on the computer screen. Silently, Natalie and Gloria read through my handiwork. Gloria smiled grimly; it was obvious she was not impressed with my efforts thus far. Natalie leaned close and whispered that I had indeed given it the correct name. She put an arm around my shoulders and reached down to pat Gloria. "Think you two could beef this up a bit?" she asked.

" . . . furthermore, negative thoughts . . . what? Beef?" Edna asked, pausing to catch her breath.

"Well, actually, Edna, we were saying—"

Edna took the ball and ran with it. "Red meat causes cancer." She then proceeded to share the atrocities that resulted from certain foods. "Peanut butter, for example. Full of fat, not to mention the oil they use to process that stuff. Might as well eat a cube of butter—which as we all know, clogs your arteries."

When she paused for a breath, Natalie was able to steer her out of the room, leaving Gloria and me to work on the script. We embraced the chance to work uninterrupted, amazed by what we were able to accomplish together. I found that my roughshod draft was plumping up into a workable play. Natalie had been right. Gloria's ideas and my limited writing capability proved to be a great combination. By lunchtime, we had achieved the impossible. A Christmas play that was cute and entertaining. As we added the finishing touches, Natalie walked back into the room to check on our progress.

"You know, I think this is going to work," she said, leaning over our shoulders to peer at the computer screen. "I knew you two could do it!" She gave us both an affectionate pat. "Now, we just need a few practices, some costumes—"

"Numerous prayers," I added, wincing as Natalie playfully pinched me.

"Nasal hairs?" Edna puffed, entering the study. "A bit unsightly, they're the body's way of filtering—"

We couldn't help ourselves. Our attempts at composure dissolved into giggles, which led to gut-wrenching laughter until the three of us were shedding tears. Looking confused and more than a little disgruntled, Edna sank onto a plastic chair. Knowing that we had offended her, we attempted to regain our composure and smooth her feathers. Natalie was the first to recover from our glee-filled lapse.

"We're sorry, Edna. What was it you were saying? Teri had just said the funniest thing."

"Oh?" Edna said skeptically. By now, Gloria and I had managed to get ourselves under control. The realization had suddenly hit that Natalie had neatly passed the buck to me.

"Uh . . ." I began.

"I heard Teri say something about nasal hairs," Edna insisted, waiting for me to share whatever it was I had said that was so obviously funny. Gloria started to snicker and turned so Edna couldn't see her laugh. Meanwhile, Natalie refused to look at me. I promised to get even with both of these women as I frantically racked my overworked brain for something funny to say about nasal hairs. All I could think of was how Mark needed to trim his on occasion.

"Teri?" Edna prompted. I could tell Natalie was getting a kick out of this. Her jaw tightened with the effort of keeping a straight face. Soon, she turned to stare in the same direction as Gloria.

"Uh, well . . . what I said was . . . that Mark's hair seems to be migrating from the top of his head into his ears and nose." Gloria started to shake violently at my side. She held one hand on her stomach while the other covered her mouth. Her back was still turned to Edna, as was Natalie's. *Chickens!* I silently jeered.

"Now, Teri," Edna said briskly, "our bodies go through changes when we get older. It's part of the aging process. Why, I'll bet you've noticed a few things about your own body lately."

Sensing Natalie's grin, I managed to poke her in the ribs with my finger. Gloria mumbled something about having to use the bathroom and made a quick exit. We all heard her laughing down the hall.

Later, after Gloria and Edna had left, I offered Natalie a Diet Coke and a ham sandwich. Before we put the sandwiches together, I grabbed my insulin out of the fridge and prepared to give myself a shot. Natalie watched in quiet fascination as I filled the syringe.

"Does it bother you to give your own injections?"

"No. Not really. It did at first . . . when I was younger."

"How old were you when you found out about the diabetes?"

"Fourteen," I said, carefully balancing the syringe to give the shot in the back of my arm. I winced as the needle slid beneath my uncooperative skin and quickly pushed the plunger in. The sting intensified, then faded as I removed the needle.

"You've been doing this since you were fourteen?" Natalie marveled, shaking her head.

"It's not so bad," I said, hoping to avoid a conversation regarding this particular subject. I silently chided myself for not slipping into the bathroom to give the shot. No doubt we would now play the game of twenty questions: *What was it like being a teenager with diabetes?* Wonderful! Doesn't every teenager want to be told they're different from everyone else? *Oh, you poor thing. It must've been awful, not being able to eat anything with sugar in it.* Yeah, well, life stinks sometimes. I imagined the rest of the conversation. It doesn't take much effort; I've had it several times in my life.

Natalie surprised me. Somehow sensing my reluctance to discuss diabetes, she gracefully changed the subject to our Christmas play. I answered her questions as I pulled out the hoagie buns and ham, and while I spread mayonnaise on the buns she sliced the ham. Our task didn't take long, and soon we were sitting at the counter, munching on the sandwiches and sipping our Diet Cokes.

"How do you think our meeting went today?" she asked as she picked up her can of pop.

"Very well," I said sarcastically. "I especially enjoyed the stimulating conversation concerning nasal hair." Natalie lost it, blowing out a mouthful of Coke, neatly spraying the top of the counter with droplets of pop. I grinned and slipped down from my stool to grab a handful of paper towels. We continued to giggle as we cleaned up the mess, then I remembered.

"That reminds me, Nat, how did you know about the doll?"

"I saw it that night I came over." She paused. "Anyway, when you guys headed back there, I wondered if you'd remembered to tuck it away somewhere."

"Well, I'm glad you thought about it. If Edna had seen it . . ." I shuddered, imagining the consequences.

"True. In a way though, I'm glad you kept it. I was tempted to take it myself. Those girls did such a good job . . . it seemed a shame to throw it away."

"Yeah, I know. Somehow, it inspires me. I'll be sitting there, struggling with a column for the paper, then I look up and see that thing. It gives me plenty of incentive to keep typing. It sounds silly, but it seems to glare at me. I can almost imagine the lecture I'd get if Edna thought I was being *slouchy* as she calls it."

Natalie smiled thoughtfully and sipped at her pop. Then she sighed and set the can on the counter. "Actually, I feel sorry for the woman. I don't think we know everything there is to know about Edna."

"Don't worry, I'm sure she'll share it all with us eventually," I sighed.

Natalie shook her head. "I'm trying to be serious here."

"Okay," I returned. "I am now shifting into serious mode." I did my best to look somber.

"She seems so sad sometimes," Natalie mused softly.

"Edna . . . sad?" I looked at her in disbelief.

"Yes. Haven't you ever noticed how she rambles on and on?"

"I believe so," I said, smiling brightly. "Like today for instance, that bit about nasal hair. Which reminds me, I no longer owe you anything, regardless of what you endured while Gloria and I were being creative."

Natalie stayed on the topic like a bloodhound. "Speaking of rambling," she gave me a disgusted look, "I don't think Edna's boys keep in touch with her like she wants us to believe."

"What makes you say that?" I asked, suddenly intrigued. Edna was always bragging about her two sons. Not to mention her seven grandchildren.

"One of my visiting teachers lives next door to Edna. The other day, she mentioned what a shame it was that Edna always spends the holidays alone."

I stared at Natalie. "You're kidding?"

"I wish I was," she replied. "I know things were pretty bad for me right then with Jerry, but I did notice there were no extra cars in Edna's driveway over Thanksgiving."

"Maybe she spent it with one of her sons," I offered hopefully.

"Nope. Her car stayed in the driveway all week. And she was at church the following Sunday, remember?"

I nodded, plagued by guilt. Suddenly, the Edna jokes seemed tacky and uncalled for.

"While we're on the subject of Edna, I want to mention something else that's bothered me for quite some time," Natalie said.

"Okay," I said, reaching for my sandwich.

"Regardless of how it might've appeared at the time, she was not called to be our secretary because of you."

I continued to chew while I waited for an explanation.

"I know you thought I wanted her around to keep an eye on you. It's not true, Teri. I thought her nursing skills would be an added plus, but, as sure as I'm standing here, Edna was called as the secretary in this organization because that's where she's supposed to be. I think she needs this calling. Just like we need each other." I could tell she was struggling for composure and I was afraid there was a hug in the making. "Teri, I don't know what I would've done if you hadn't been there for me that night."

"Oh, I didn't do that much," I said, trying to discourage her from giving me undue credit.

"If you hadn't taken the time to listen . . ." She wiped at her eyes. "Anyway . . . things are better now. And I have you to thank for that."

"Is it better, Natalie?" I asked. I knew what an actress this woman could be. Problems like Jerry's don't disappear overnight.

"I would be lying if I said it's perfect at home," Natalie said slowly. "There are still times when Jerry loses control. When he snaps over trivial things."

My expression must've given me away. Natalie seemed to know exactly what I was thinking. "Teri," she said softly, "it isn't like you think. He *is* doing better. The counseling has helped. But we have a long way to go. And, just so you know, he hasn't laid a hand on me . . . at least, not like . . . you know." She blushed. I smiled, enjoying her embarrassment. At the same time, I was relieved to know her relationship with Jerry had improved. "You'll never know how much I appreciate your friendship," Natalie said, reaching for that hug I had sensed was coming. Somewhat awkwardly, I patted her shoulder.

"Now, we have to help Edna," Natalie said, pulling back and looking at me earnestly. "She needs us, just like I needed you. I felt that so strongly today. If you could've seen the look on her face when we were out here visiting in your kitchen . . . "

"Okay," I groaned."You've sold me on it. Tell me what I can do to help."

Her smile told me I'd probably live to regret whatever it was.

Chapter 9

During the week of the Christmas pageant, last-minute costume crises were an everyday occurrence. The snowman costume from last year was too small for this year's snowman. One of the shepherds refused to wear a robe in public. During a rehearsal, an angel managed to fall off the stage, ripping a hole in her mother's new white sheet. Mark made several bad jokes about our "fallen angel," but I ignored him.

Using my limited clout, I gave Hank the starring role of Joseph in the nativity scene. He was thrilled until he began worrying about his costume. Concerned that his mother would make him drop out if any cost was involved, I assured him we would round up an ensemble. I made a few calls, located several possibilities, and invited him over one afternoon. A brown robe fit Hank perfectly. I grabbed a beige-colored towel to complete the outfit. Mark tied it in place around Hank's head, and we stepped back to survey the results. Hank looked very much the part of a solemn Joseph.

His eyes were bright with excitement as he studied his reflection in the bathroom mirror and we stood in the doorway. "Can I wear the costume home to show my mother?" he asked after numerous thank-yous. We knew he was hoping she'd come watch the production. For his sake, so was I.

As the play came together, we realized we had forgotten the annual Primary gift-wrapping ordeal. Every year, a portion of the Primary budget is used to purchase a small gift for each child in the ward. Once purchased, the small toys and gifts to be handed out by Santa needed to be properly wrapped and tagged.

Natalie came up with the idea of grouping the gifts together in classes instead of families as was the usual custom. We would start with the babies of the ward, then work our way through the Nursery, continuing through the eleven-year-old Valiants. Our fearless leader was convinced this would not only be quicker and smoother, but would also ensure that we'd have a gift for every child. She reminded us that the previous year an entire family had been forgotten. Luckily, the former Primary presidency had had the foresight to wrap a few extra gifts. However, a disgusted eleven-year-old girl had received a toy truck while her four-year-old brother had been given a necklace. The presidency had forgotten to designate the gender intended with the extra gifts.

We agreed to learn from the mistakes of the past presidency. We'd already put word out that if there were any visiting children coming to this event, their relatives or parents were to furnish gifts for Santa to hand out. Confident we had covered our bases, we met one night at the church to begin the infamous wrap session.

We'd all brought snacks to munch on, anticipating a lengthy evening. I took Natalie aside to ask if Jerry was okay with her spending so much time away from home. She smiled and told me that Jerry was taking their kids out for pizza, then home to watch the Christmas videos she had rented earlier in the day.

I was amazed by the changes that were taking place within the Cox household. Natalie was rapidly becoming a close friend and confidante. I wanted her to be happy, and judging by the look on her face tonight, she was currently ecstatic.

Natalie had already organized the gifts into appropriate groups, so we started by wrapping the gifts. The boys and girls in each class were to receive the same thing. For example, the three-year-olds were getting kaleidoscopes, boys and girls alike. The ten and eleven-year-old girls were receiving small diaries. The boys that same age would be given wallets with varied designs. Most of the gifts had been ordered from Oriental Trading, a mail-order company that sells bulk items relatively cheaply. We split up the gifts according to class and wrapped each group of gifts in the same kind of paper to avoid confusion. To save the ward money, Edna had purchased the Christmas wrap and tape on sale at a discount store. It wasn't until that night we realized why the tape was on sale. Not only was it barely sticky enough to hold the paper together, but the dispensers contained razor sharp metal teeth. It didn't take long for each of us to become the recipient of a grievous puncture wound. But in the spirit of Christmas, we restrained our criticism. After nearly thirty minutes of wrapping bliss, we were startled by a loud obscene cry from our secretary. We stared at the small trickle of blood sliding down her thumb. The poor woman looked so mortified by what she'd said, we all hastened to her side to offer sympathy and assistance. Ever prepared for an emergency, Natalie pulled a Band-Aid out of her purse and handed it to Gloria, who set about administering first aid to Edna. Natalie then slipped me her church keys, giving me the assignment to find the rolls of transparent tape kept in the library. Only too happy to comply, I hurried down the hall.

To salvage her pride, Edna pointed out how nice the presents looked after they were wrapped, mentioning again how much money she had saved by purchasing the Christmas wrap on sale. Natalie silently indicated we should agree with the woman and we complimented Edna on the extra effort she had made on our behalf.

As we attached the appropriate tags, Natalie led the conversation, asking each of us what our plans were for the holidays. I knew where she was heading with this. It was a tactful way of finding out if Edna would be spending Christmas alone.

"So, Teri, you mentioned your sister and her family would be coming up from Salt Lake to spend Christmas with you and Mark. Sounds like fun."

"Yeah. I can hardly wait. Have I mentioned the pet names we've given her four-year-old twins?"

"They're boys, right?" Natalie asked.

"Last time we checked," I replied. Gloria grinned while Edna frowned her disgust.

"All right, let's hear'em."

"You're brave," I responded, smiling at Natalie. "Here goes. Thing One and Thing Two. You know, from Dr. Seuss' *Cat in the Hat*?"

"Thing One and Thing Two . . . weren't those the two little creatures who tore the house apart?" Natalie questioned, lifting one eyebrow.

I nodded. "See why I'm so excited?"

Natalie laughed and reached for the list of names Edna had typed. "Gloria, what about you? What are you doing over the holidays?"

"Well, Ian and I were planning on spending a romantic Christmas at home. It would have been the first one together. And probably the last one we'd spend with just the two of us for quite a while." From her tone and our previous conversation at my computer, I gathered that Gloria wasn't exactly thrilled over the prospects of motherhood.

"But . . . ?" I prodded.

Gloria met my questioning gaze with a sad smile. "Ian's mother is insisting we spend Christmas with them."

"Can't you tell her you appreciate the invitation, but would rather spend it alone this year?" I asked.

"Ian's already caving in. He told me last night how much fun we could have in the Wyoming snow."

"That's where your in-laws live?" I asked, scratching another name off the Primary list.

"Yeah. Ian grew up on a ranch in a small town called Alpine," she said, looking unhappy at the prospect of a Christmas with her in-laws. She also didn't look like she cared to continue the conversation and focused her attention on the present she was wrapping.

Natalie looked thoughtfully at Gloria's face as if making a mental note to follow up with her later in private. For now, she shifted the conversation to Edna. "Edna, what are your plans for Christmas this year?"

Edna avoided Natalie's probing gaze and continued writing names on the tags she'd gathered. "Oh, I suppose both of my boys will be upset with me again this year. I want to spend a quiet Christmas at home. They always want me to travel to spend it with them, but I don't enjoy flying. Never have. Makes me air sick. Not a pleasant thing, air sickness."

Unwilling to let the conversation slide into airborne maladies,

Natalie stubbornly steered Edna back to the subject at hand. "Where do your boys live?" she asked.

"Ed and his wife and four children live in Detroit," Edna answered matter of factly. "Jake, his wife and three daughters live in Tallahassee."

"Clear down in Florida?" Gloria asked, her eyes widening.

"I know. Every time I get my phone bill, I say to myself, I say, Edna, you ought to take Jake up on his invitation and move down to live in Tallahassee. I'd still be a considerable distance from Ed, but he usually makes it down to see his brother at least once a year. Idaho, of course, is so far away. It's next to impossible for them to get here as often as they'd like to." She sniffed loudly. Trying to be subtle, I waited a few seconds before turning to look in her direction. She'd taken her glasses off to wipe at the lenses. I met Natalie's worried glance and knew her suspicions had been correct. Edna would be spending another Christmas alone. No invitations had been extended, and I was certain her sons wouldn't be coming to Idaho.

Edna replaced her glasses, mumbled something about needing to use the rest room, and disappeared down the hall.

"You know, it's too bad Edna won't fly out to see her boys over the holidays. No one should spend Christmas alone." It was obvious Gloria had missed what was really going on. But, then again, I had been blind to it myself until Natalie had enlightened me.

"Gloria, Edna won't fly out to see her boys because they don't want her there," Natalie said in a hushed voice, keeping an eye on the door.

"What?" Gloria exclaimed. "She's their mother. Why wouldn't they want her to spend—?" We both gave her a funny look. It finally clicked. "Oh. Well . . . maybe she is a little annoying," Gloria shrugged. "But she's still their mother."

"I know," Natalie sighed. "This has been going on for years, though. I'm not sure what caused the initial problem, but when I asked the bishop about it a couple of weeks ago, he said both sons have made it perfectly clear they don't want anything to do with Edna."

"That's terrible!" Gloria said, echoing my own sentiments on the matter.

"Remember two years ago when she fell and broke her leg?" Natalie asked.

I nodded at the same time that Gloria shook her head. The accident had happened before she had moved into our ward.

"I was serving as the Compassionate Service leader at the time. Our Relief Society President, Sister Knight, tried to contact both sons. She finally got through to the one in Detroit. He said it was a real shame, but he wasn't in a position to do anything about it. He said that was what the Relief Society's for, and hung up."

"You're kidding?" I said, totally disgusted. When Natalie shook her head, I felt my blood pressure rise. "I don't care how irritating she can be, she deserves better than that!"

"True. Which is why I think we should try to contact her sons again. It is Christmas, after all. You'd think they'd be willing to forgive past grievances. Holding grudges doesn't get anyone anywhere." I nodded. If anyone understood that concept, it was Natalie. "I did manage to get Ed's number from Bishop Anderson," she continued. "He's all in favor of us trying to mend the fences between Edna and her sons. Wouldn't it be great if we could talk them into coming to Idaho Falls for Christmas this year? Can you imagine how excited—" just then, a grim-faced Edna walked into the room—"how excited these children are going to be when Santa arrives with all of these gifts?" Natalie said, thinking quickly.

"Yeah. They'll be so hyped up for Christmas, their parents will personally want to thank each of us," I said lamely, in an attempt to help Natalie. She flashed me a grateful look before smiling at Edna

"Oh, Edna, you're back. Good. We need to separate these gifts into different bags, label them with the appropriate class name, and we're finished," she bubbled. It was amazing, watching the woman in action. Natalie could handle just about any situation smoothly. Edna obediently grabbed the white plastic trash bags we'd brought to stash the gifts in and began helping us sort. It wasn't long before everything was finished, the table was cleared of debris, and the bagged gifts were hidden inside a large canvas bag in the Primary closet. Natalie locked the closet door, then looked at all of us. "We did get everyone a gift, right?"

Edna pulled out the official Primary list and scanned it. "Yes. Every name has been crossed off."

"And we remembered all of the babies in the ward?"

Edna scowled. "The records are in order. Every child has been accounted for."

"I know, Edna, and we sure appreciate the work you do for us. But I can't shake the feeling that maybe tonight, in the confusion of wrapping, we—"

"Every name has been crossed off," Edna said stubbornly.

Natalie smiled. "Well, okay then. We're done. I'd like to thank all of you for helping with this project tonight." We gathered our things and followed her out of the Primary room.

Edna pulled out of the church parking lot in her tan Honda Civic, followed by Gloria in a green truck. Natalie would take me home in her car. As she unlocked the car, I knew something was troubling her and decided to take the bull by the horns. "What's up, Nat?"

"I don't know. For some reason, I have this nagging feeling that we've forgotten someone."

"Oh?"

"Would you mind if we double-checked the bags?" she asked, giving me a wistful smile.

"Tonight?" I asked as I peered in the darkness at my watch. It was already after ten.

"I know it's late. I'll have to call Jerry and explain. I'm just not sure we'll have another chance to check. And I'd feel terrible if we left somebody out."

"Okay," I said, feeling slightly irritated. Edna was certain we'd covered every child, and I was confident in her bookkeeping skills. On the other hand, I could see that Natalie would stew over this until it was settled. I reluctantly followed her back to the church, fighting an overwhelming desire to go home, change into my pink fuzzy robe, and sip at some sugar-free hot cocoa while my husband gave me a foot massage and sympathized over the puncture wounds in my thumbs.

"I really appreciate this, Teri," Natalie said as she hung up the phone in the hall. Jerry had evidently given his approval. Defeated, I followed Natalie into the Primary room. "I'd slip down tomorrow and do it, but Kimberly's kindergarten class is putting on a Christmas program in the morning. Then I'll have her with me the rest of the day. I'd have to answer a million questions concerning Santa's gift bag—"

"I get the picture, Natalie," I said as I slipped out of my coat. "Let's hurry and get this over with."

Natalie lifted an eyebrow over my lack of enthusiasm.

"Do you have a list of the children?"

She nodded and pointed to her canvas tote bag. "Will you find the list while I get the bag of presents. I agreed, curious to see what I'd find in Natalie's bag and eager to do some snooping. I already knew what the rest of us carried around in our Primary bags. Edna filled hers with notebooks, records, roll cards, pencils, scratch paper, and a small spray can of Lysol. Gloria's bag contained a binder haphazardly filled with Scouting paraphernalia and the Primary Handbook, a notebook, antacids, and saltine crackers. My bag holds a Primary Handbook, a blank notebook for last minute brainstorms, a couple of pens, the ideas for Sharing Time I'm continuously collecting from relatives and acquaintances, and the usual assortment of candy and juice I keep with me at all times. Now, as I sifted through Natalie's bag, I could see it was as organized as everything else the woman had contact with. Her Primary handbooks and records were neatly compiled in a large binder. Everything was alphabetized. It didn't take long to locate the list of children.

"Here it is," I said cheerfully. I don't pout for long, despite what Mark thinks. I knew Natalie was only trying to do her best in this calling. And, I had promised to support this woman. "Let's start with the babies," I suggested, glancing at the list in my hand. Nearly thirty minutes later, we had gone through every plastic bag, crossing off names as we sorted. Every child had been accounted for.

Natalie sighed, shook her head, and smiled apologetically at me.

"I'm really sorry about this. I guess I'm paranoid. I want everything to work out perfectly, and I'm afraid I'm going to mess up."

"No problem," I said as I helped her replace the white plastic bags inside of the canvas Santa bag. "As for messing up, quit worrying. We're as ready as we'll ever be. What could possibly go wrong?" Little did I realize I would be eating those words in a very short time.

Chapter 10

"You're sure this is the right number," I asked, listening intently to the phone. The frail connection continued to ring. "Five, six . . ."

"I'm positive it's Ed's number. Let it ring a couple more times," Natalie begged.

I smiled grimly and glanced at the clock in my kitchen.

"Seven . . . eight . . . I don't think anyone's home, Nat. Oh. Hi there. Is this Mrs. Ed . . . I mean, Barrett?" As Natalie snickered behind me, I turned and gave her a dirty look.

"What are you trying to sell me," the voice on the other end of the line said sharply.

"I'm not trying to sell anything. Please, don't hang up. I'm calling about your mother-in-law, Edna Barrett."

"Has something happened?"

"No, no, she's fine. I'm not sure how to say this . . . I . . . there's someone here who can explain it better than I can." I grinned and handed the phone to Natalie. She made a face at me, then slipped immediately into a gracious mode.

"Hello, Mrs. Barrett? Yes, well, this is Natalie Cox from Idaho Falls. I'm in the same ward as your mother-in-law. . . . No, she's fine. A little unhappy though . . . that's why we're calling. Teri, the woman you just spoke to, and I both work with Edna in the Primary Presidency. . . . No, Edna's my secretary, I'm the president. Teri's my first counselor. Anyway, we've gotten to know Edna quite well. She's not one to complain but . . . oh, I see. Well, maybe we haven't known her long enough but she . . . no, she's never said anything negative about any of you. Just the opposite. She's always commenting on what fine sons . . . if you'd let me explain . . . please, don't hang up. We called because we're worried about her. She seems so lonely. We were wondering . . . since it's Christmas . . . oh, I see. It must make things difficult for you. I know, she can be a little exasperating on occasion, but she means well. Is there any chance . . . I see. Could you at least give me Jake's number? I promise I won't tell him where I got it." Natalie gestured for a pen and some paper. I grabbed my purse off the counter, sorted through the contents, and quickly handed her both items. "Thanks," she mouthed as she hurriedly scribbled down a phone number. "Thank you, Mrs. Barrett. I really appreciate it. And would you please mention this call to your husband when he gets home? It would mean so much to Edna if . . . no, she didn't put us up to this. But she seems so down this Christmas . . . I realize that, but still, isn't there any way . . . ?"

From the one-sided conversation, I picked up enough to have a pretty good idea of what was being said. I couldn't help it—I had reached my boiling point with these people. Grabbing the phone away from Natalie, I seethed with self-righteous indignation. "Look, Mrs. Barrett, this is Teri Patterson again. I don't know what the problem is here, but would it really hurt to call once in a while? You people should be ashamed of yourselves! How many years has it been since any of you have seen Edna? She is Ed's mother after all. Don't you have any kind of consideration for . . . hello? Hello?" I glanced sheepishly at Natalie and handed her the phone. "Sorry. I guess I slightly lost my temper," I mumbled.

"It's okay," Natalie sighed as she gazed at the paper in her hand. "I wasn't getting anywhere with her anyway."

"They seem pretty intent on keeping their distance. Did Ed's wife say why they don't stay in touch?"

"Not really. Something about Edna making their lives miserable for years and they're tired of it."

"I guess we'll get the same response from Jake," I murmured.

"Guess so," she replied. "Still, it wouldn't hurt to try."

"True."

"I do have one suggestion," she added with a smile. "This time, let me do the talking," she said as she reached for the phone.

"Hello? Jake Barrett? I'm sorry if our timing's a little off. Your wife said you were about to head out the door. . . . No, this isn't a sales pitch. I'm calling about your mother. . . . No, she isn't dead. She's very much alive. . . . Why am I calling then?" Natalie gave me an exasperated look. "Look, Mr. Barrett, this is Natalie Cox, from Idaho Falls. Your mother serves with me in the Primary presidency in our ward. . . . No, she's the secretary. I'm the president. . . . No, I don't consider that to be a blessing. Edna would make a wonderful president. Anyway, as I was saying, your mother has been a little down lately. . . . You're wrong, this does concern you. It's nearly Christmas and we were wondering . . . what do you mean, we who? . . . No, this isn't a ward conspiracy!"

I could tell Natalie was losing her patience, a rare occurrence. As her face flushed with frustration, I suspected she was about to explode.

"We're calling as her friends and we thought . . . no, she didn't complain about you! We're worried, okay?! She's so lonely. . . . I doubt it was her choice. Whatever the woman did, isn't it time to let bygones be bygones? She's not getting any younger. One of these days, she may not be here, and, speaking from personal experience, it's better to settle these things while you still have the chance. . . . I do understand. My husband recently lost his father . . . there was a lot of bad blood between them. It nearly destroyed Jerry . . . my husband. What do you mean this has nothing to do with you? It has everything to do with you! Your mother cried the other night because she's so miserable!"

I sensed Natalie had reached her breaking point and snatched the phone out of her hand. "Hi there, Jake. Can I call you Jake? This is Teri, Jake. I'm another one of your mother's friends. Natalie was about to have a stroke, so I decided to step in. . . . Yeah, she's a regular little hothead," I agreed, moving out of her reach to continue the conversation. "Look, Jake, we can discuss this like two rational adults, can't we? Good. We're concerned about your mother . . . yeah, she's quite a character. Well, like I was saying, Edna hasn't been acting like herself lately. . . . No, I don't think that's a good sign. . . . Yes, she really cried the other night. We were discussing our plans for Christmas and . . . no, I'm not trying to put a guilt trip on you. I realize that . . . but, you know, I think sometimes we forget how much our mothers love us. . . . Oh, come on now, Jake, Edna loves you. You ought to hear how she always brags about you and your family. . . . No, seriously. We had no idea there was even a problem until one of Edna's neighbors mentioned your mother always spends the holidays alone. We thought maybe this year for Christmas . . . I see. I know it's expensive. Could you at least give her a call? Or write a letter? Anything to let her know you care. . . . What do you mean, that's the problem? You do too care. Jake, we all say things we don't mean . . . I'm sure that was merely her way of . . . don't hang up . . . please, Jake. Please? Hello, Jake?" I shut off the cordless phone and handed it back to Natalie. "Jake had to go. We've made him late for his bowling tournament."

"Bowling, huh?" Natalie said as she hung up the phone. "How thoughtless of us."

A mild form of depression settled in as Natalie and I sat quietly pondering what to do. After a few moments, Natalie slipped down from the stool to the floor. "Well, we tried. I guess that's all we can do." She sighed and walked into the dining room to retrieve her coat. I followed her to the entry way. "Dang it, Teri, I really thought this would work!"

"I know," I replied.

"If Jerry and I were going to be home for Christmas, I'd invite Edna to spend it with us."

"Yeah, well, I think it's more important for you guys to make this trip." The Cox family was going to California to see Jerry's mother. Natalie had explained that their counselor had recommended this holiday visit so Jerry could make peace with his father. Jerry planned to visit his father's gravesite where he had been "assigned" by the counselor to get a few things off his chest. It had something to do with the healing process. I didn't completely understand it, but if it would help Jerry to continue making progress, I was 100 percent for it.

"It'll be so hard for me to enjoy this trip, knowing Edna is sitting here alone."

"Hey, no problem. Mark and I would love to have her come over for Christmas dinner." How had that slipped out? Mentally, I kicked myself. I knew Mark would finish the job when he found out what I'd agreed to do.

"Oh, Teri, would you?" Natalie reached over and pulled me close for one of her infamous hugs. "You don't know what this will mean to Edna, and to me."

Nevertheless, I had a pretty good idea of what it meant to Natalie. This was the most intense hug I had ever endured in my life. When she finally let go, I gasped for air and forced a smile, even though I felt more like crying. Thing One and Thing Two and Sergeant Edna? Was I into self-torture these days or what?

Mark took it better than I had thought he would. He seemed to think we would be embracing the spirit of Christmas by having Edna over Christmas Day. I didn't agree, arguing we would be embracing disaster, but, I was stuck. Not only had I promised Natalie, but, she, in her great rush of excitement, had already called Bishop Anderson with the good news. He later called to thank me for being such a compassionate person. It was a good thing he couldn't see the look on my face. Compassion was the one expression I wasn't wearing.

Mark felt we should make a personal visit. So, taking advantage of the unseasonably warm weather, we walked over to her small brick home. She invited us in and escorted us to a couch encased in a plastic slipcover. I shouldn't have been surprised, knowing the woman as I do. We sat very carefully, but each time we moved, embarrassing noises resounded loudly, compliments of the plastic. Mark tried not to laugh as I jabbed him in the ribs with my elbow. We sat rigidly in place, leading up to the reason for our visit.

" . . . and we were wondering if maybe you'd like to have Christmas dinner with us next week?"

Edna sat quietly in the plastic-covered wingback chair. I had thought she would jump at the invitation immediately, but I was wrong. It proved to be a long, drawn-out affair with Mark and I practically groveling for the honor of her presence.

"I don't know, dear. I was looking forward to spending a nice, quiet day here at home."

"We promise not to keep you all day," Mark encouraged. "You could come and go as you like. But we'd really love to have you over for dinner."

"Well, there's my boys. They always call on Christmas Day. If I'm not here, they'll be frantic. They're always so worried about me. Two years ago when I broke that leg of mine, I never had a minute's peace. Those boys called around the clock to check on me."

"Let them know you'll be spending the day with us," I offered, trying to be helpful. Besides, I thought, if her sons knew she was spending Christmas with one of the ladies who had called them to repentance, maybe their consciences would plague them.

"I don't know. My boys are always saying I'm so hard to catch. It'd be my luck to be over at your house when they call."

With a sudden rush of insight, I knew what Edna feared. She was hoping her sons would call. She was afraid that if she left, she'd miss the call if it came. I felt a tug at my heart. As I fought to maintain my suddenly fragile composure, Mark came through with a wonderful idea.

"I've got it," he said, snapping his fingers. "We'll bring over our answering machine and hook it up to your phone. We'll leave a message on it to let your sons know where you are and when you'll be home." He beamed, looking rather pleased with himself.

"I hate those machines myself. They always sound so impersonal. I hang up when one of those things takes off a jabberin'. Maybe my boys would do the same."

I could see it was going to take some big-time convincing to sway the woman. "Now, Edna, I'm sure your boys will call back if . . . I mean, when they hear the message on the machine. This way, you could have dinner with us and . . . uh . . . when they call back later, you'll still get to talk to them."

"Well, I guess you have a point. No sense in staying here if you really want me to come to your place for dinner." Her eyes revealed how much she wanted to come. "You say it would be fairly simple to hook up that answering machine?" she asked hopefully. Mark assured her it would be no problem. Her piercing gaze settled on me. "Now, then, young lady, what can I bring to help with dinner?"

"Oh, don't worry about it. My sister is coming up the day before Christmas. She's a regular gourmet. We'll . . ."

"I insist on bringing something," she said stubbornly. "In fact, I won't come unless you let me."

I finally gave in and slid back on the couch, temporarily forgetting the plastic slipcover. I sent Mark a look that made it perfectly clear I was not amused by the unfortunate noise that had resulted from my shift in positions. Edna, caught up in deciding what to bring, didn't let on that she'd heard anything.

" . . . or, I could make pumpkin pies. Ed used to love my pumpkin pies. And . . . wait a minute. You couldn't eat anything like that," Edna said, gazing at me with concern. "Maybe I'd better—"

"If you'd like to bring a pumpkin pie, that's fine, Edna. I usually indulge in a few treats over the holidays." Was that ever the wrong thing to say! We spent the next fifteen minutes enduring a stern lecture on the evils of diabetics who stray from the straight and narrow. When she finally finished, even Mark was ready to swear off sweets.

" . . . instead, I'll bring a nice Jello salad. They make sugar-free Jello these days, you know."

"I know," I murmured.

"A sugar-free salad it is. That would be much better."

I merely nodded, picturing the mouthwatering delicacies my sister had planned to make, treats I would have to avoid this year. The wonderful concoctions that made Christmas dinner enjoyable and worth enduring Thing One and Thing Two. Since our parents had left last November to serve a mission, Debbie and I had been taking turns hosting the traditional family gathering. Last Christmas, we had gone to Debbie's house in Salt Lake. This year, my home would be invaded. Mark's parents were spending Christmas in Arizona with his sister's family. His parents rotated each year. Last year, they had spent it with Mark's brother's family. Next year, they would be spending it with us. Something to look forward to. Mark's mother was a wonderful cook. Maybe I could sample holiday cooking next year.

Mark poked me with his finger. "Edna was just saying how wonderful this was of us," he said as he smiled at me.

"It'll be great having you there," I heard myself say. We slid forward, ignoring the protesting plastic, to stand. It was time to go home.

Later, as I soaked in the tub bemoaning my sad fate, I remembered the look on Edna's face. The hopeful expression as she had talked about her sons calling on Christmas Day. Ashamed of my selfishness, I vowed to make this the most successful Christmas dinner ever. I wanted it to be so good, it would soften the blow when Ed and Jake didn't call.

Chapter 11

The night of the ward Christmas party had finally arrived. I changed three times before settling on a red dress that was not only an appropriate holiday color, but was also one of Mark's favorites. He'd given it to me for Christmas last year, commenting that red was definitely one of my colors. It must be, considering how often I embarrass myself.

I slipped into the dress and glanced in the mirror. I gazed at my reflection, focusing on my hair. I'd taken so much time deciding what to wear, I hadn't left much time to primp. Hurrying into the bathroom, I threw on some makeup and curled my hair. The extra effort was worth it; Mark whistled his appreciation when I finally emerged from the bathroom. I returned his smile, impressed by how attractive he looked in his grey tailored suit and red tie. Earlier in the day I had swallowed a tiny portion of pride and had ironed his best white shirt. The man looked sharp. Arm in arm we proudly left the house, anxious to show each other off.

We pulled up in front of Hank's apartment building a few minutes later. Mark slipped out of the Blazer to race up the stairs and knock at the door. When he returned with Hank, I was delighted to see that Hank's mother had chosen to come as well. Hank opened the car door and Mark gallantly helped Sylvia Clawson into the Blazer. She smiled self-consciously at me, then glanced down at the faded pair of jeans she was wearing.

"I didn't know . . . Hank didn't say this was a formal thing," she stammered as Hank climbed in beside her. "If we have time, I could change." She nervously fingered the small camera she had brought.

"You're fine," I said, assuring her that only the Primary Presidency had chosen to dress up for the occasion. Everyone else in the ward would be dressed casually, except for the Primary children. Those who weren't wearing costumes were supposed to come wearing their Sunday best. I wondered if everyone would remember to dress appropriately. Then I wondered if the children would remember their lines. I was just starting to wonder if our Santa Claus would show up when Mark climbed in and told me to quit worrying. He smiled at Sylvia, telling her what a nervous wreck I had been all week. Mark has a way of calming people who are ill at ease. Sylvia returned Mark's smile and seemed to relax. As for myself, I was no longer nervous, I was mad. Contrary to popular belief, I was not a nervous wreck! A bit concerned that things wouldn't go as smoothly as we had planned, but definitely not a nervous wreck. As I stewed over Mark's comment, I began chewing the nails of one hand. Hoping he hadn't noticed, I quickly folded my hands in my lap.

I couldn't stay mad at Mark for very long. Within minutes, his unique sense of humor had us all laughing as we turned the corner to the church house. Hank excitedly hopped onto the sidewalk as Mark helped Sylvia and I out of the Blazer. Together we walked toward the large brick building.

Natalie had arrived a few minutes ahead of us and was bustling around with her usual efficiency. The spotlight had already been moved into position. Even the Christmas tree lights had been plugged in. All that remained was for our cast of Primary kids to show up. I paced the floor, trying to calm the butterflies that were having a hey-day in my suddenly delicate stomach. Natalie finally steered me out of the cultural hall and into the Primary room for a brief chat. On our way, she gathered Gloria and Edna.

"I want you three to know how much I appreciate everything you've done the past few months," she said, gesturing to three corsages laid out on a small table. "Merry Christmas!"

"Natalie," I protested, thinking of the cost, "you shouldn't have done this."

"You deserve more, but I didn't have time to come up with anything else. Enjoy!" She handed us the festive corsages that were made up of three miniature white carnations decorated with tiny red ribbons and backed by shiny green fern. Gloria pinned Edna's on while Natalie helped me. As Natalie moved to help Gloria, I noticed Edna had removed her glasses to wipe at her eyes. Edna then cleaned her glasses, complaining that the winter weather always managed to steam them up.

Smiling brightly, Gloria pulled out three small packages from her Primary bag. She carefully handed them out, instructing us to wait until Christmas to open them. Natalie gave her a big hug. I settled for saying thanks.

"I left my bag in the other room," Edna said, clutching Gloria's gift in her hand. "Stay put, I've got something for each of you."

"I think you started a trend," I murmured to Natalie as I moved toward my own bag. I reached inside and pulled out three beautifully wrapped boxes of candy. "Sweets to the sweet," I said as I passed them out.

Gloria beamed with pleasure. She'd been craving candy lately. "Thanks, Teri. This is so thoughtful of you, especially when you can't . . ." she paused, suddenly uncomfortable.

"It's okay, Gloria. Just because I'm supposed to stay away from this stuff, it doesn't mean the rest of you have to."

Natalie gave me the anticipated hug, effectively smashing my corsage. She suddenly gasped and pulled away. Turning her back to me, she pressed a hand against her chest.

"Nat, are you all right?" I asked, stepping forward.

"Yeah," she whispered. "I think I just skewered myself on your pin."

I tried not to laugh, but couldn't help myself. For once, Natalie's hug had proved to be a bigger pain for her than me.

Edna reappeared, puffing with the exertion of hurrying into the cultural hall and back. She reached into her bag and pulled out a handful of crocheted pot holders. A set for each of us. They were the same color as our individual kitchens. Natalie's were yellow, mine were green, and Gloria's were orange. Touched by what she had done, we thanked her enthusiastically.

"Didn't have time to wrap 'em," she wheezed as I handed her the box of candy. She nodded her thanks, and placed it inside of her Primary bag.

"Well," Natalie said as she glanced at her watch, "it's almost show time. We'd better head back to the cultural hall."

"Special delivery!" a loud voice boomed. We stared as Jerry entered the room carrying a clear plastic container. Inside was one of the most beautiful white rose corsages I have ever seen. Natalie was stunned. "You didn't think I'd let my best girl be the only member of the presidency without a corsage," he said, winking at me. He smiled at his wife's shocked expression, opened the plastic box, and held out the corsage. "Anyone care to pin this on her?" he asked, glancing around.

"Go for it, Jer," I said impishly as I shooed the other women out of the room. When I reached back to close the door, I caught a glimpse of Natalie sweeping her husband off his feet with one of her exuberant hugs. And this time, she didn't gasp, he did. Another pin had found its mark.

Our Christmas production went well, all things considered. We only had two casualties. Three-year-old Nancy Martin had chosen to delve into the depths of her nose with a finger while nervously lisping through her small speaking part. The frantic gesturing by her mother and teacher failed to capture the young girl's attention until a small trickle of blood began running down Nancy's finger. Certain she was dying, Nancy began to scream accordingly. The girl's mother hurried forward to help her daughter off the stage and into the rest room down the hall.

Another moment of embarrassment occurred a few minutes later. It happened when our snowman decided to throw himself into his dancing routine. He whirled wildly around, lost his balance and fell over, his back toward the audience. The seams of that too-snug suit gave way, splitting out in front of the entire ward. The poor boy was devastated beyond words. He ran off the stage and spent the remainder of the program hiding in the boys' rest room. We did manage to coax him out before Santa made an appearance.

When it was time for the nativity scene, I was so proud of Hank's wonderful performance of Joseph. I glanced over at his mother, who dabbed at her eyes as the children sang the final number, "Silent Night." Then it was over. The weeks of preparation had paid off. The program had been a success. After the closing prayer, eager ears listened for the tell-tale sounds of Santa. They weren't disappointed. Ringing a string of bells, the jolly man in the red suit ran up and down the aisles, belting out several hearty "HO-HO-HO's."

The kids were ecstatic. They watched in excited delight as Santa took his place on the stage sitting in a large chair beside those of us in the presidency. He set down the large canvas bag, took the microphone from Natalie, and began to call out the names of the children as we handed him the gifts. He explained that this year, the gifts would be handed out in Primary classes and started with our youngest members of the ward, the babies.

The children seemed delighted with the small gifts we had selected. The idea of distributing gifts by class worked like a charm. As one class stood up to walk onstage, another class returned to their chairs to tear open the packages from Santa. Edna had volunteered to gather paper and began to collect the discarded Christmas wrap from in front of the stage and between the rows of chairs.

Santa kept things moving along and quickly passed out gifts as Natalie, Gloria and I removed them from the white plastic bags. We'd finally come to the gifts for Hank's class. I was thrilled his mother was here to see what a wonderful Primary organization her son belonged to. Thrilled, until a panicked look on Natalie's face revealed something was very wrong. She leaned to whisper the cause of concern and soon my expression matched hers. There was no gift for Hank. I couldn't believe it, but somehow, we had forgotten him. Natalie frantically searched the white plastic bag again. She handed it to me and I searched. We were running out of time and options; Santa had already distributed most of the gifts, and confident that we had a gift for everyone, we hadn't bothered to wrap extras.

I glanced down and saw that Sylvia Clawson was making her way to the front of the stage, camera in hand. Two children were ahead of Hank. What were we going to do? Closing my eyes, I prayed for a miracle.

Suddenly, I had a flash of inspiration. I leaned close to Gloria and explained the dilemma. Then I asked what she had given us for Christmas. She gave me a funny look and whispered her reply. Somewhat relieved, I reached behind my chair for my Primary bag. Thank heavens I had brought it onstage! I'd felt nauseated earlier and fearing a reaction was on its way, had kept the bag close with its usual stash of candy and juice. I quickly pulled out the gift from Gloria. I knew she wouldn't be very thrilled, but, under the circumstances, we didn't have much choice. I pulled off the tag and handed it to Natalie, quietly urging her to give it to Santa for Hank. Natalie gazed at me, then, realizing our backs were against the wall, did what I asked.

Santa visited with Hank for a few minutes, encouraging the boy to sit on his knee while Sylvia took a picture. Hank smiled shyly and gratefully took the gift from Santa's hand. He grinned at his mother, then at me, and hurried off the stage to unwrap his present. I crossed my fingers, held my breath, and prayed this would work.

The other boys his age had received colorful hacky-sac balls. They had already torn open the packages and were bouncing the vinyl balls off themselves and those unfortunate enough to be sitting nearby. When Hank opened his gift, he stared at the object in his hands. Turning, he gaped at Santa.

"This isn't working, is it?" Natalie whispered. I was about to agree when Hank jumped up from his chair, handed the gift to his mother, climbed on stage, ran ahead of the kids waiting in line, and gave Santa a big hug. Then, grinning, he hurried back to his mother.

Relieved, we helped Santa through the rest of the gift-giving ordeal. No one else had been missed. After the last gift had been handed out, and the final Christmas wish list shared with our visitor from the North Pole, we cheered as he disappeared from the cultural hall, ringing his bells in one last joyous clamoring. It was over, and despite everything, we had survived. It was time to pick up the pieces and go home.

Gloria was exhausted. We convinced her we could handle cleaning up the cultural hall and sent her home with her husband. She was still feeling terrible that I had given up my gift. I told her not to worry about it. The look on Hank's face had been the best present I'd been given in a long time.

As Natalie and I began taking down the decorations, Sylvia Clawson approached. Mark had mentioned he would run Sylvia and Hank home, then return to help us clean up.

"I couldn't leave without thanking you ladies," Sylvia stammered. "How did you know?" she asked, tears filling her eyes.

"Know what?" I asked, puzzled.

"That tiny glass globe with the snow scene. It's beautiful. Hank saw one like it the other day at the mall. He kept staring . . . he even shook it once to watch the snowflakes settle. I wanted to get it for him, but I . . . ." She paused, her face flushing with embarrassment. "Anyway, I wanted you to know how much tonight meant to him. Thank you." She hurried away before Natalie or I could respond. We stood in silence for several seconds, absorbing what had just taken place.

After the chairs had been put away and the floor had passed Sergeant Edna's inspection, we sat in the Primary room and went over the records with our secretary. Sure enough, Hank's name was missing from the list we'd been using. Somehow when Edna had typed up the list of children from the official church record, she had skipped right over the nine-year-old. Edna felt horrible until we told her how well things had worked out. She mumbled something about the Lord working in mysterious ways and offered to give me her gift from Gloria. I declined, convincing her Gloria would be hurt if she even considered giving that gift away. I then reminded her Mark would be picking her up at ten o'clock on Christmas Day. She had insisted on coming early to help with the dinner. Edna smiled, grabbed her bag, and left the room. Mark and Jerry were waiting for us in the lobby. Natalie sighed and picked up her bag as I retrieved mine from a nearby corner.

"Well, I guess that's it," she commented.

I agreed, reminding her she still had to pack for their trip. They were leaving for California in the morning.

"We're already packed," she said as she flipped off the light.

"I should've known," I mumbled as we walked down the hall.

"Thanks for saving us tonight," she said with a smile. "You were certainly inspired."

"You're the one with the inspiration," I insisted. "You tried to tell us we had missed somebody."

"I know. That nagging feeling pestered me for the longest time. But, we'd checked the list thoroughly. We had even double-checked the bags."

"Makes you kind of wonder if it was supposed to turn out like it did," I said, remembering the look on Sylvia's face.

"It certainly does," she agreed. "It also makes you count your blessings. I can't imagine how hard life must be for Hank and his mother. I always assumed Sylvia didn't come out to church because she was bitter over the divorce. Maybe there are other reasons. She puts in long hours at work . . . and she has to work some weekends. I learned that much when I served as the Compassionate Service Leader. Sylvia didn't want visiting teachers. We thought she was becoming inactive, but maybe it was because she has such limited spare time, or didn't want to be reminded of what life is like for the rest of us."

I nodded and wondered if it was too late to do something special for Hank and Sylvia for Christmas. Later, as Mark and I curled up beside the fireplace in our living room, I explained the situation and told him what I'd like to do. He grinned and pledged his support, adding a few ideas of his own.

Chapter 12

On Christmas Eve our fair city was dusted with a layer of snow. By nine o'clock the flakes were huge, falling in a slow, lazy pattern to the ground. I loved it. As Mark and the ward members who had offered to help with *Operation Santa* loaded our Blazer and Ed Bergen's Suburban with boxes of gifts and food, I danced around, trying to catch as many flakes as I could with my tongue.

"You're a kid at heart," Mark teased. He wrapped his arms around my waist, squeezing the breath out of me.

"You love it and you know it," I countered, patting his arms.

"I know. I love the snow. I love Christmas Eve. I love what we're doing tonight. And most of all—"

"I know, I know, you love your dear, talented, beautiful, affectionate—"

"Computer!"

I wiggled free to glare at him. Then I walked off, pretending to be hurt.

"Oh, come on, you know who I meant," Mark panted as he caught up to me. He pulled me close, lowered me dramatically toward the ground, and planted a juicy kiss on my protesting lips. Cheers and whistles permeated the air.

"Looks like Teri and Mark are getting into the spirit of things," a loud voice exclaimed.

I blushed and pulled away from Mark, wondering why the bishop had chosen that moment to show up, dressed as Santa. Behind Bishop Anderson stood Shauna, his wife. Great! They had witnessed Mark and I in one of our finer moments. If this kept up, we'd have quite a reputation in our ward. Natalie was still giving me a bad time about the pillow fight.

Bishop Anderson continued to grin and made a smart remark about crossing mistletoe off our wish list as we obviously didn't need it this year. Mark laughed and tried to drape his arm around my shoulders. I pulled away after pinching him a good one. He continued to chuckle and walked over to shake the bishop's hand.

"Nice outfit," Mark commented.

"Isn't it though?" Bishop Anderson quipped.

"I thought it would be a good idea. This way, if someone sees us, they won't be frightened," Shauna explained.

"Good thinking," I replied, returning her smile.

The bishop motioned for everyone to gather around. As we assembled in a semi-circle, he asked Mark to offer a prayer. After the prayer, we hurried off to accomplish our deeds of good will.

There were four families in our ward who were short of funds this year. As Mark and I had tried to quietly gain support for our own Christmas venture, Joni Morgan, the current Relief Society president, had caught wind of what we were doing. We weren't the only ones intent on spreading holiday cheer. Generous quantities of food and gifts had already been gathered for the four families, including Sylvia and Hank. We combined our efforts and were now trying to sneakily distribute the boxes of goodies that had been collected.

Our first stop went off without a hitch. We parked down the street to avoid detection. Santa and his little helpers grabbed four boxes and carried them down the sidewalk. They deposited the boxes on the front porch of a tiny house and with a gusty "HO-HO-HO!" rang the doorbell and fled. They hid around the corner of the house as the rest of us rolled down our windows and strained for a glimpse at the front door. A young man appeared and stared at the boxes. His wife slipped out beside him. Their only child, a two-year-old girl, had had open heart surgery two months ago. Little Clarice was doing well and had been able to come home for Thanksgiving, but her parents were facing overwhelming medical bills. Santa had heard that their Christmas would be very meager this year. We were touched when Clarice's mother called out her gratitude. "Thank you, whoever you are!" she exclaimed. We watched in joyous silence as the boxes were gathered and taken inside. The warmth in our hearts lingered after the door was quietly shut.

Our next stop was not as successful. This time our object of intent was a widower named Emmett Hunt. The feisty sixty-eight-year-old lived alone, somehow managing on the small monthly pension he received. He consistently refused help, claiming he didn't believe in charity. He didn't come to church very often, and those times when he did, most wished he'd stayed home. He was ornery, rarely saying anything of a polite or positive nature. Extremely critical of most Church leaders, especially those in our ward and stake, he was a constant challenge to the priesthood brethren. Still, it *was* Christmas, and we were determined Emmett would have something to enhance the holiday. It was doubtful he would ever express his appreciation. We would be lucky if he didn't toss the box out into the street, but we had to try.

Moving as quietly as possible, Mark helped the bishop carry the box to Emmett's doorstep. Then, braced for the worst, Mark pushed the doorbell. He and Santa raced around the house as a shotgun blast shattered the silent eve.

"Dad-blamed hooligans! Come out here where I can see ya!" Emmett snapped angrily, lowering his shotgun.

I nervously swallowed and prayed Emmett's aim was as off as he was.

"Show yerselves, ya rotten no account delinquents!"

I gasped as Santa made an appearance. There was no sign of Mark. I panicked, opened my door, and slid to the ground to cautiously make my way down the street.

"Merry Christmas, Emmett Hunt," Santa boomed loudly.

"Merry what?" the man demanded, aiming his gun at Santa.

Suddenly, Shauna Anderson appeared at my side. We exchanged a worried glance and continued to move forward.

"Merry Christmas!" Santa insisted, standing his ground. "And shame on you for being a Scrooge."

"Keep talkin'," the old man threatened, cocking the gun.

"Shut up and live, dear," Shauna said under her breath. I

glanced at her grim face, then stared at the scene transpiring before our eyes. Where was Mark? Shauna grabbed my arm and gestured toward the side of the house. Mark was peering around the corner at Bishop Anderson. I breathed a sigh of relief and tried to move closer, but Shauna held me back.

"I think he's bluffing," she whispered, pointing to Emmett. "Besides, it might upset him more if he sees Harvey didn't come here alone."

Harvey? Bishop's real name was *Harvey?* To the best of my knowledge, everyone had always called him Bud. Bishop Bud Anderson. I made a mental note to add Harvey to the title. Bishop HARVEY Bud Anderson. It might make up for the mistletoe crack he'd made earlier.

I followed Shauna's lead and moved across the street to stand behind a large tree in someone's front yard. Someone who was obviously not home. I wondered if we could break in and call for help if it was needed.

"You have a pretty poor Christmas attitude," Santa commented.

"I'll give ya plenty of attitude, compliments of old Bessie, here," Emmett warned, patting his gun. "Now, you just come pick up this box of trash and be on yer merry way!"

"Emmett, that box is for you. Take it in the spirit it was intended."

"No sir! I don't take handouts from nobody."

"Not even Santa Claus?"

"You ain't Santa! Yer a sorry excuse of a man out pokin' his nose in private affairs! Now, git this charity box outta here before I blow a hole clean through it and you!"

"You wouldn't shoot Santa, now would you?" Bishop Harvey Bud Anderson pleaded.

"Don't tempt him, dear," Shauna said, biting her lip.

Two little boys suddenly appeared out of nowhere. They ran down the street, calling for Santa. Emmett turned to look at them and cursed.

"Don't shoot Santa Claus, Mr. Hunt," one boy hollered. "He still has to come to my house," he added, running up to the front porch of Emmett's house.

"Git outta here," Emmett shouted, lowering his gun.

"Please, Mr. Hunt," the younger boy pleaded. As he ran into view, I recognized him. Nathan Phillips, a six-year-old member of our Primary. The other boy was Cole Phillips, Nathan's eight-year-old brother.

"Did he hurt you, Santa?" Nathan asked, shyly stepping closer to Bishop.

"No. Santa's fine," Bishop said cheerfully.

"Why is Mr. Hunt trying to shoot you?" Cole asked, giving Emmett a dirty look.

"He doesn't want his Christmas presents," the bishop explained.

"Why?" Nathan asked as he glanced back at Emmett. "Santa's supposed to bring us presents," he explained. "But only if we're good. Have you been good, Mr. Hunt?"

"Sure he has," the bishop said before Emmett could open his mouth.

"That's why Santa came to see you," Nathan insisted, walking back to stare up at Emmett. "You should be nice to him."

"Bah! You brats don't even know what Christmas is about!" Emmett snarled.

"Do you?" Cole asked.

"'Course I do!" Emmett snapped. There was an uncomfortable pause as the two little boys continued to stare up at him. "Go on, git home. What you starin' at?"

"But . . ." Cole started.

"I said git! Your mamma's probably worried sick wonderin' where you're at."

"She doesn't know we're here. She thinks we're asleep. We climbed out our bedroom window when we saw you try to shoot Santa," Cole revealed.

"Why do you want to shoot Santa?" Nathan repeated. "It's Christmas."

"Christmas don't mean nothin'!" Emmett growled.

"It does so. It's Jesus' birthday. Mom says we give gifts to each other cause we can't give them to Jesus," Cole informed Emmett. Again, there was an uncomfortable pause. Emmett finally gave up and stomped inside his house, slamming the door behind him.

"He's mean," Nathan said, looking at the bishop.

"He's not mean, he's lonely," Bishop Anderson replied. "Now, if you two want me to visit your house, you'd better hurry home and fall asleep."

"'Kay," Nathan said excitedly, running off.

"Merry Christmas," Cole shouted as he eagerly followed his brother home.

"Merry Christmas," the bishop called after him. Turning, he slowly trudged away from Emmett's house.

"What about the box?" Mark asked quietly. Shauna and I had moved to our husbands' sides to offer comfort and moral support.

"We'll leave it," the bishop said. "Emmett's a proud man. He won't take it inside as long as we're here to see it." The bishop was right. Later, after the deliveries had all been made, Mark and I drove back to see if the box was still on Emmett's porch. It had disappeared and hopefully had been taken inside. Regardless, we had tried.

Our next stop was down the street for a family of eight, Roger and Penny Burch and their six children who ranged in age from fourteen years to eighteen months. Roger had been laid off from a furniture factory during the summer. He had applied everywhere he could think of, but at present, was still unemployed. His wife had taken a temporary job at a department store during the Christmas rush. Her employment ended the last week of December. Roger was now thinking of moving his family to Utah, hoping to find work. We all ached for the family. We knew the same thing could happen to any one of us at any time with the economy as unstable as it was.

We had planned to leave six boxes on the Burch porch. Earlier in the day, the bishop had rounded up a couple of extra boxes of food and gifts, bringing the total to eight. It took every one of us to carry the bulging load. Our sagging spirits soared as we successfully deposited the boxes, rang the doorbell, and hid around the corner of the house. Penny answered the door, then stood crying as Roger came out behind her. He glanced at the boxes and held his wife close, sharing in her tears. Quietly, we crept away, unwilling to intrude on this emotional scene.

Our final destination was the Clawson residence. Mark and I had purchased nice sweaters for Hank and his mother. We had also picked out a small racetrack for Hank and a necklace with matching earrings for Sylvia. People in the ward had donated two boxes of food, including a large ham for their Christmas dinner. The other gifts were wrapped and we had no way of knowing what secrets the brightly colored paper held, but felt confident they would be appreciated and well received.

Bishop Anderson, Mark, and Ed Bergen each toted a box up the stairs that led to the small apartment Hank shared with his mother. The bishop waited until Mark and Ed had made it to the parking lot before ringing the doorbell. He then belted out a hearty "HO-HO-HO!" Someone parted the curtains to peer out. It suddenly occurred to me that Sylvia, living alone as she did with Hank, might be reluctant to answer the door. But, when Hank heard the bishop call out the traditional Santa greeting, he bolted out of the apartment before Sylvia could stop him. He hugged Santa, then gaped at the boxes.

"Are these for us?" Hank shyly asked.

Santa nodded.

"See, Mom," Hank hollered as he grinned at his mother. Sylvia had hesitantly moved into the doorway. "I told you Santa would come. I prayed about it. See, he came! He really came!"

Shauna Anderson began to softly sing, "We Wish You a Merry Christmas." Soon, the rest of us joined in. Hank and his mother couldn't see us; we kept ourselves out of sight, but later, when we gathered at the bishop's house for hot chocolate and doughnuts, he told us how Sylvia had burst into tears, begging to know who we were so she could repay our kindness. The evening ended as it had begun, with the excitement of Christmas clasped within our hearts.

Chapter 13

Christmas morning we were awakened by the delighted squeals of my nephews as they discovered Santa had indeed found them in Idaho Falls. This had been quite a cause of concern for Eric and Derek. The four-year-olds had expressed this worry on a frequent basis during the past forty-eight hours. Debbie and her husband, Rick, had patiently reassured that Santa would find them. Mark and I had backed them up, hinting that Santa actually preferred to deliver gifts in Idaho Falls as compared to Salt Lake where he had to fight the smog. Debbie had given me a dirty look, but I had chosen to ignore it, only too happy to enlighten my nephews with these little-known facts.

As I lay in my soft, warm bed refusing to budge, I wondered what delights the day would hold in store. I didn't have to wait long. Mark, with an enthusiasm shared by our nephews, forced me out of bed and downstairs to join in the fun. Our living room was already a disaster area. Shredded Christmas wrap and bows were everywhere. I moved an empty box from my favorite chair and watched as Eric and Derek opened the last of their treasures from Santa.

Debbie handed a beautifully wrapped box to Rick. He sat on the carpeted floor and excitedly opened it, pulling out a gorgeous blue sweater.

"I suppose you crocheted that," I said with a sigh. Debbie could do everything—cook, sew, make awesome gifts out of items other people throw away. Debbie, the competent, beautiful, big sister who had always been greatly envied by me, the younger, less attractive klutz. I hoped that somewhere, somehow, in the great scheme of things, it would all balance out. I would someday be recognized as a writer of great distinction. My trial in life would be finding enough room to display the awards that would be thrust upon me.

"Actually, I knitted it," Debbie replied, jarring me back to reality.

"I love it, Deb, thanks," Rick beamed, pulling it on over his pajama top.

I controlled the urge to mention what a trendsetter Rick was. The striped pajama top clashed horribly with the sweater, but Mark still looked on with envy. I was tempted not to give him the special gift I had picked out weeks ago. Then, overcome by the thrill of giving, I hunted under the tree for the box I had stashed earlier in the week. I finally found it and handed it to Mark. He took a deep breath and tore into the paper with gusto.

"This is so great," Mark murmured as he pulled out a colorful box.

"What is it?" Debbie asked.

"Lazerwarp!"

"Lizard what?" Rick asked, trying to step over Eric to move in for a closer look.

"Lazerwarp," Mark repeated. "It's a new computer game. I've dropped hints for weeks," he added, grinning at me. "Thanks, Teri," he said, sealing his joy with a wet kiss on my cheek.

"Here Deb," Rick said, handing my sister a small box. I lifted an eyebrow. Rick had either gotten cheap in his old age, or Debbie was about to receive a bit of jewelry. I should've known it would be the latter. Rick had given her diamond earrings with a matching pendant.

"Wow!" I commented, glancing over Debbie's shoulder. Debbie couldn't speak but the tears that were shed communicated volumes. Rushing across the littered room, she hugged the stuffings out of my brother-in-law. I gazed at Mark, imagining how thrilled I would feel to receive such a gift.

When my sister regained her voice, she told Rick that the best gift was still under the tree. Crawling across the crowded floor, she pulled out a small box about the size of the one Rick had just given her. Were they on the same wave length this year, or what? I gazed at the gift in her hand, wondering if it was a ring or a watch. It was neither. A stunned Rick pulled out a small envelope. Giving his wife a quizzical look, he opened it, read the contents of a tiny card, and whooped with supreme joy. He lifted Debbie into the air, whirled her around the room, hugged her close, and kissed her long and hard.

"Daddy, put Mommy down!" Eric commanded, looking up from the large metal dump truck he was playing with.

"Yeah, Daddy, put Mommy down!" I echoed. I was dying to know what Debbie had given to cause such a reaction. Whatever it was, I wanted to get something similar for Mark.

"Okay, okay," Rick said, obediently lowering his wife to the ground. "This is the best gift I've ever had," he added, grinning from ear to ear.

"Out with it already," I said.

"Yeah, what's the deal?" Mark asked.

"I'm going to be a daddy again!" Rick proudly admitted.

"What?" I questioned, turning to look at Debbie. Debbie slowly nodded, the joy in her eyes changing to concern as she returned my gaze. I forced back an undesired wave of longing and gave my sister a hug. "Congratulations, Deb," I murmured. She held me close for several seconds. I finally pulled away to let Mark congratulate her and gave Rick a squeeze. "Way to go, big guy," I said brightly. Mark grinned and pumped Rick's hand enthusiastically. Then, clapping his hands to get our attention, Mark informed us he had an announcement of his own.

"Your attention please. I am about to present my jewel of a wife with the only Christmas gift she's never been able to figure out."

Mark had a point. Every year, mostly by chance, I always manage to discover what he's picked out for me. Two years ago, I had pulled up just as he'd entered the house with a guitar case in hand. Last year, I had walked into Chesbros to search for some sheet music and had walked by a keyboard I had admired for weeks. The tag indicating it was sold had come as quite a disappointment. Then I noticed Mark Patterson's name was on the tag. It wasn't my fault things like that always happened to me—but try convincing my husband.

Last Christmas, I had put on an academy award performance acting shocked, but Mark had not been amused or fooled. Instead, he vowed to surprise me next year if it killed him.

As we waited to see what Mark had stashed away this Christmas, I gazed at my sister's jewelry and was suddenly convinced I would receive a similar offering from my husband. Mark had given an obvious hint. Jewel of a wife—anyone could've figured it out. As I braced myself to feign astonishment, Mark entered the room carrying a bird cage. I didn't need to feign anything. I stood in place with my mouth open as a small parrot began to express its dismay which was as genuine as mine.

"His name is Bogey," Mark said, handing me the cage.

"What?" I asked, feeling as though the wind had been knocked out of me.

"He's so . . . cute," Debbie offered, trying to be polite.

"Is it named after the actor?" I murmured, trying to be a sport.

"No, the golf term," Mark informed me, "and he's not an it. This poor little birdie was discovered on a golf course by one of my customers." He waited for us to laugh at his intended pun, but the only one who even attempted a smile was Rick. Giving up, Mark continued with his explanation. "They kept him for a few months, then came home one day to find that their puppy was carrying him around in his mouth. They decided to find Bogey a new home and . . ."

"And I think we know the rest of the story," I said, sinking into a chair. I set the cage on my lap and stared at the green-colored bird on the perch. He squawked noisily which did nothing to lift my spirits. As I continued to stare, I spied a tiny gift-wrapped box on the floor of Bogey's cage. I glanced at Mark and could tell he was enjoying this immensely.

"Got ya!" Mark chuckled.

I hesitantly opened the cage and reached for the gift. It was at this time Bogey decided to share his displeasure with me. Disgusted, I pulled out my hand, set the cage on the chair, and hurried into the bathroom to wash off the fresh dropping. A few minutes later, I rejoined the chortling group in the living room. Bogey was now perched on Derek's shoulder and was busy trying to preen my nephew's blond hair. Debbie smiled at me and Rick tried not to laugh as once again, Mark held out the cage. I gave them each a dirty look and reached inside for the other gift. I quickly unwrapped it and pulled out a beautiful watch. "Oh, Mark," I said in a hushed voice. "It's gorgeous!"

"I knew you needed a new one, but thought I'd make you wait until Christmas," Mark said.

"And the bird?" I asked, giving him a hug.

"Actually, we're bird sitting. His owners went to Arizona for a month. We have to give him back in February."

"Oh, darn," I said as I shared a relieved smile with Debbie. She shook her head and sat next to Rick on the couch. Mark and I sank into the love seat and watched the boys play with their new toys for a while, then began to gather the paper and boxes. It was already 9:00 a.m. We only had an hour before Mark was to pick up Edna.

True to form, Edna had been eagerly waiting for Mark to arrive. When they returned to our house, Debbie let them in, grinning at me as Edna walked through the dining room holding out the green, sugar-free Jello salad she had insisted on bringing. I sighed and set the salad in the fridge, finding it a spot next to the cheese ball Debbie had made last night. When I had told my sister about Edna, she had graciously agreed to fix only those things that I could eat without concern. Edna would be proud. There would be no sweets served today.

With Debbie's help, I stuck a ham in to bake. Then, under the close supervision of Edna, we made oyster dressing—one of Mark's favorites, double-baked potatoes, asparagus served in butter sauce, dinner rolls, and for dessert, cream puffs filled with sugar-free pudding. Edna agreed to stuff the celery sticks I'd cut up earlier with a variety of flavored cheese spreads and arranged them on a platter while I sliced dill pickles and drained the water from two cans of olives. It would be a feast fit for a king, or in this case, Dame Edna. And the beauty of it was, I could sample everything without feeling guilty. As we set the table, I practically drooled with anticipation.

Eric and Derek had been quite well behaved most of the morning. They argued during an intense game of Operation, but Mark quickly settled it by offering to play it with them. He even managed to talk Rick into participating. It was their way of helping us. With all four boys out of the way, we were able to have dinner on the table by 1:00 p.m.

Everyone gathered around our oak table. We had added the extra leaves, so there was plenty of room. Mark was seated at the head of the table. Debbie sat to his right with Eric sitting next to her. We'd placed Edna on the other side of Eric, figuring she would act as a deterrent to his usual hyper behavior. Rick sat across from Debbie, and Derek was seated by his side. I sat at the other end of the table across from Mark. Mark asked Rick to offer the blessing on the food, and soon after the prayer, we began passing around the bowls and platters of food, heaping generous quantities onto our plates. We were so engrossed in consuming the delicious meal, we didn't notice that Bogey had chosen to join our ranks. I looked up just in time to see the parrot fly into the dining room. Mark had told me Bogey's wings had been clipped. This was obvious from the way the parrot tried to pathetically project itself into our midst. After a near disastrous landing on the china cabinet, Mark jumped up and tried to rescue the silly thing. Bogey didn't want to be rescued. He wanted to be where the action was. He flew over Mark's head, this time aiming for the table. One foot managed to cling to the chandelier as he passed by. Looking like a trapeze artist, Bogey swung around the fragile metal arm, then crash-landed on top of Edna's head. Edna shrieked and I quickly reached for the insubordinate bird. As I lifted him from his current perch, taking great care to untangle his feet from the unruly hair, Bogey dropped a deposit. Horrified, I handed Bogey to Mark and glared at my brother-in-law who was trying not to laugh. Debbie gave her husband a similar look, then hurried into the kitchen for a handful of paper towels.

"Bogey dropped—" Eric started. I slipped my hand over his mouth.

"A gob of—" Derek added before Rick could stop him.

Edna, suddenly catching on, glared at me and stomped down the hall to the bathroom.

"All right," I hissed as Edna closed the bathroom door. "Who left Bogey's cage open?" Derek refused to look at me. I shook my head as Debbie slipped an arm around my shoulders.

"Sorry, Sis," she murmured. "I'm sure Derek didn't mean for this to happen."

"It's okay," I mumbled. "Things were going too well. I should've known something like this was in store."

Edna suddenly reappeared, looking as feisty as ever. I braced myself for the worst. What would it be? A lecture on the germs that had no doubt been spread by Bogey? The unsanitary practice of having live animals in the house? Instead, Edna surprised me. She sternly marched into the dining room, then burst out laughing. Before long, we joined her, chuckling over the outrageous incident. During the remainder of the meal, we shared other embarrassing moments from our various lives. Edna added a few that had occurred while she had worked as a nurse. Edna was actually a riot. I couldn't believe it was the same woman I worked with in the Primary.

After we cleaned up the kitchen, Edna agreed to stay and play a game of Scategories. While Eric and Derek watched a new video they had been given, compliments of Mark and me, the rest of us gathered around the dining room table and played two rounds of the word game. Edna was a formidable opponent and won the second game. We then played a lengthy game of Monopoly, which Rick, the real-estate whiz, won hands down. Next, we helped ourselves to another chocolate-filled cream puff and sat down in the living room to visit.

When it was about 7:30, Edna, who had been having such a good time, suddenly realized how late it was and insisted on going home. We begged her to stay and watch "It's a Wonderful Life," but she refused. I knew she was anxious to see if anyone had bothered to call in her absence. I prayed that was the case, but had a feeling Edna was in for a disappointment.

She thanked us for allowing her to spend the day, gathered her things, and left with Mark. Debbie and Rick put their sons to bed while I popped up some microwave popcorn for our movie. We planned to start the video after Mark returned.

He reappeared nearly thirty minutes later with Edna. Puzzled, I followed him into the kitchen after he had settled Edna in the living room.

"There were no messages," he said quietly. "She was so upset . . . I talked her into coming back with me."

I nodded, glad that Mark had convinced Edna to return. None of us would've enjoyed what remained of the holiday, thinking of her alone and sad. I grabbed the big bowl of popcorn and walked into the living room with a smile plastered on my face. Determined to restore the cheer we had felt earlier, I started the movie and passed the popcorn around. Soon, we were all rooting for Jimmy Stewart as we learned again that it was a wonderful life.

Chapter 14

It didn't take much effort to convince Debbie and Rick to stay a few extra days. Rick was on vacation anyway, and Mark had some vacation time coming. Both felt a male bonding session was in order and excitedly made arrangements to take a snowmobile trip through Yellowstone Park. Something they had wanted to do for years. They tried to talk Deb and I into joining the adventure, but when we considered Debbie's current condition, not to mention the problem of what to do with Eric and Derek, we declined. Debbie and I were looking forward to spending some time together. Besides, there were sales to check out now that stores everywhere were trying to reduce their inventory before the end of the year.

Two days after Christmas Mark and Rick left early for their trip. I sleepily bid my husband farewell before he slipped out of the bedroom. He kissed me soundly and asked me to promise to behave in his absence, which I refused until he promised to be careful. Then, as he made his way down the stairs, I rolled over and dozed off. When I woke up later, the sun was shining brightly and the inviting smell of fried bacon lingered in the air. Debbie must have fixed breakfast. *Good for Deb*, I thought as I snuggled under my warm covers.

"I was beginning to wonder if I needed to check for a pulse," Debbie complained, walking into the bedroom.

I stuck out my tongue, threw back the covers, and sat up.

"Sales wait for no woman," she lectured as she reached for my robe.

I stood, took the robe from her hand, then slowly sank onto the bed as a paralyzing wave of nausea hit me.

"Teri, are you all right?" Deb asked, moving to the bed.

Groaning, I stretched out across the quilt at the foot of the bed.

"I gather that's a no," Deb said, feeling my forehead. "No fever," she said. I ignored her, realizing it was the mothering instinct. "Do you need juice or a candy bar?"

"I don't know. Grab my monitor. It's on the dresser."

Debbie obediently hurried across the room and returned with my One Touch. She'd done this often enough through the years. With smooth efficiency, she helped me run a quick check. "It's 145."

"That's pretty good."

"I know. Now what?"

"I'm not sure. Unless it's on its way down. Sometimes my levels drop fast."

"Good point. I'll go grab something for you to nibble on."

She left the room and I slowly slid around until my head was on my pillow. I couldn't believe this was happening. Debbie and I didn't get the chance to do things together very often. Mentally cursing, I tried to block out the nausea.

"Here, try some of this," Debbie encouraged as she walked to the bed with a glass of orange juice in her hand.

I lifted my head for a sip. Debbie forced me to drink half the glass before she'd let me ease back onto the pillow.

"Feeling better?" she asked.

"No," I whined, closing my eyes. If anything, the nausea was worse. I suddenly sat up and covered my mouth with a hand. "Get me into the bathroom quick!" I demanded. Debbie helped me out of bed, and I bolted for the toilet, barely making it in time. Debbie disappeared, then knelt beside me with a freshly dampened wash rag. I shakily took it and wiped my mouth.

"All right, Teri, level with me. Is it the flu . . . or what?"

"I don't know," I admitted, leaning against the wall.

"You seemed fine last night."

"Nights are better," I said. "I've had some tiny tummy twinges off and on for a while. For some reason, it's worse this morning.

I'm sure it's just the flu."

"How long is 'a while'?" Debbie pressed.

"A little over two weeks."

"Why didn't you say anything about it earlier?"

"I had so much going on. That series of articles I had to finish on downtown's Christmas Bazaar. Then there was the Primary program. Plus you guys were coming and my house was a total disaster. *And* Mark and I had to help with Operation Santa."

"I get the picture. But you could've told me if you weren't up to company. We could've made other plans."

"Deb, I wanted you to come. And I was really looking forward to the next two days. Dang it! Why does this rotten body of mine always have to have the last say?"

"C'mon, let's get you back to bed," Debbie said as she helped me to my feet.

"I don't feel as bad now," I said hopefully. "Maybe later we could still . . ." I didn't have the energy to finish the sentence.

"We'll see," Debbie replied. She guided me to the bed and covered me with the quilt. "I'll go make some toast. Maybe some tea. Do you have any on hand?"

"Mark bought some caffeine-free herbal stuff last month. He claims it helps his sinuses."

"Good. I'll hurry. In the meantime, you relax."

I tried to relax, but a few minutes later, two pairs of curious eyes were staring at me. "Hi, guys," I mumbled to my nephews.

"You okay?" Eric asked, stepping closer to the bed.

"You sounded like Mommy," Derek added, standing next to his twin.

"What?" I asked, glancing at Derek.

"She throws up a lot too. She did this morning after Daddy left. Then she ate some toast. It makes her feel better."

"Do you have a baby in your tummy?" Eric asked as he continued to stare.

"What?" I stared at him, aghast.

"Eric!" Debbie scolded as she shooed her sons out of the room.

"You heard?" I said weakly.

"Yes," she admitted. "And he's not the only one wondering."

"Oh, right! Get real, Deb."

"It *is* a possibility."

"No way!" I shook my head defiantly.

"Quit arguing," she said, handing me a piece of toast.

"There's nothing on it," I grumbled.

"Butter will make it worse," she said firmly as she sat on the bed, carefully balancing a hot cup of herbal tea. "Eat!"

I hesitantly took a tiny bite. Then another. It tasted wonderful. And the funny thing was, it actually seemed to make a difference. My stomach didn't feel as cantankerous. I slowly sat up, took the cup from Debbie, and sipped the tea.

"You're getting some color back in your face," Debbie commented.

"See, I just needed to eat. I'll finish this tea and we can still hit those sales."

"I don't think so," Debbie replied.

"Deb—"

"Teri, we need to figure out what's going on with you. This could be serious."

"I'm not pregnant, okay. Mark and I have discussed this and we've been very careful."

"Nothing's foolproof. Are you on schedule?"

"What?"

"You know what I mean. Are you?"

Realizing I wasn't, I groaned and thought of Sally. "This can't be happening."

"I think it is, Teri," she said, looking concerned. "You've got every sign. When do you see your doctor again?"

"The middle of January."

"What's his name?"

"Doctor Moulton."

"I think we need to set up an appointment today."

"Even if he's in today, which I doubt, he's so busy, we'll never get an appointment. He's booked weeks in advance."

"We need to try. Is his number written down somewhere?"

"Yes, but—"

"Teri, we need to know what we're dealing with. If this has been going on for a couple of weeks, something's obviously wrong. You're sick and we're going to find out why." She gave me a look I've often shared with Mark. Stubbornness must run in our family. Giving up, I took a bath while Debbie called my doctor.

As luck would have it, Doctor Moulton was in and when my overly excited sister explained what she thought was the problem, he worked me into the day's schedule. I now had an eleven o'clock appointment, thanks to Debbie. By the time I had dressed, combed my hair, and thrown on some makeup, I was feeling ridiculous.

"Debbie, this is silly. Maybe it was something we ate last night. That pizza did taste a little funny. Maybe the cheese was bad or—"

"You're going and that's final," Debbie said as she hung up the phone. She'd called Edna to see if she was up to a session of babysitting. Edna had offered her services Christmas night. "If you need someone to look after those two rascals, I'd be more than happy to oblige," Edna had said. "You four ought to go out to dinner somewhere," she'd added with a smile. Now, she was tickled to death that Debbie had taken her up on the offer.

"What did you tell her?" I asked, fearing the worst.

"I told her we were going to hit a few sales," Debbie replied, "and then go to lunch somewhere. If everything turns out like you seem to think it will, we'll do both, so it's not a lie," she stressed. My sister has never been one to lie, another annoying trait we'd inherited from our mother.

"Okay," I said glumly. I wanted to go shopping, not sit around in a doctor's office all day. Suddenly, I had a brainstorm. "Hey, wait a minute. Why don't we run to the drugstore and get one of those kits. We could find out now. And when it's negative, I'll call Dr. Moulton, cancel the appointment, and we can go shopping."

"If it'll make you feel better, we'll go get a kit. But, by the time we buy it, bring it home and try the stupid thing, we'll be late for your appointment."

"What time is it?"

"Ten fourteen," Deb said after glancing at her watch.

"Oh. Never mind," I said, doing my best imitation of Gilda Radner.

With a flourish that reminded me of Natalie, Debbie quickly cleaned up both of her sons and helped them on with their coats and boots. We then headed to Edna's house. Edna beamed with pleasure, only too happy to guide my nephews into her uncluttered domain. I grinned at the thought. It wouldn't stay uncluttered for long.

A few minutes later, we found ourselves in the crowded waiting room in Dr. Moulton's office. I thumbed despondently through the pages of an outdated magazine. I just wanted to get this whole thing over with. I wouldn't even let myself begin to believe that I might, in fact, be pregnant. Finally my name was called.

"You're coming with me," I told Debbie. "This whole thing was your idea."

"You can change in here," the nurse said, opening the door to tiny examination room and handing me a blue flowered gown.

"You're kidding!"

"Since a potential pregnancy for a diabetic can be serious, the doctor's going to want to examine you," the nurse replied before she left the room.

"Oh, lovely," I said, glancing at Debbie.

"Stop pouting. It's part of the process. The joys of being a woman."

"Quit rubbing it in. The only thing that makes me feel better is knowing you recently endured this humiliation yourself." I turned my back to her and quickly changed. I didn't want Dr. Moulton to walk in before I was clothed in the less-than-adequate gown.

After Dr. Moulton was through poking and prodding, he insisted on a urine test and complete blood work up.

"I'd like to look everything over and make sure before I tell you the results," he said. "Can you come back in a few hours?"

As we left the office, I fumed, "Isn't that just like a man? They thrive on controlling every situation!"

"He wants to be completely sure," Debbie said in an attempt to placate me.

"No," I said. I felt almost as irritated with Debbie as I did with Dr. Moulton. "He knows. I could tell by the look on his face. All I've done today is waste his time and mine."

"It wasn't a waste, especially if we can find out what's going on." She led me out of the room and down the hall to the small lab in Dr. Moulton's office. They wanted to check the accuracy of my monitor today to rule it out as a source of concern. It didn't take too long, and soon we were on our way.

Debbie offered to buy me lunch to cheer me up. We went to a Chinese restaurant and ordered combination dinners. As the waitress disappeared with our order, I went into the ladies' room to give my shot. I balanced the bottle of insulin on the sink after I'd drawn what I needed into the syringe. As I turned around to give the shot in my hip, I brushed against the sink and knocked the bottle of insulin onto the floor. It shattered on impact. I cursed under my breath, finished giving the shot, and reached for a paper towel to clean up the mess.

"You okay in there?" a familiar voice asked.

"Go away," I said, furious at Debbie and myself. Furious with life in general. And terrified of what Doctor Moulton would tell me later. What if I was pregnant? Would the baby be all right? Would I make it through the pregnancy? On the other hand, what if I wasn't pregnant? Could I handle another false alarm? Three years ago, I'd been so sick, everyone had assumed I was pregnant. Mark had been so hopeful. It had devastated him when we later learned it was my appendix acting up.

"Teri?"

"I'm okay," I lied, wiping my eyes. "I dropped my insulin bottle and naturally it smashed all over the floor."

"Let me in. I'll help you clean it up."

"I've got it," I replied, gripping the pieces of glass in a paper towel.

"Don't cut yourself," she warned.

The warning came too late. I was already bleeding. But the wound was only visible to me.

Chapter 15

After lunch, we hurried to the Grand Teton mall to check out the sales. As we tried on outrageous outfits in an attempt to outdo each other, I began to relax. The next two hours were quite enjoyable. Holiday canvas shoes caught Debbie's eye and we each bought a pair. Bright acrylic stones decorated the now-out-of-season shoes. Debbie's were arranged as a series of Christmas lights, each acrylic stone a different color. My shoes displayed tiny wreaths that were covered with small acrylic stones. We sat down on a bench to put them on, slipping our boring *normal* shoes into the plastic bag we'd been given at the shoe store. Then we bought Christmas sweatshirts to match our shoes and changed quickly in the rest room.

Ignoring the stares from those around us, we next went to the toy store to find something for Eric and Derek. When I held up two noisy laser pistols, Debbie violently shook her head.

"Aw, c'mon, Mom, have a heart," I whined, imitating a boy we'd run into on another aisle.

"Nope." Debbie said firmly. "You only have to listen to them for a couple of days. I'm stuck with them forever," she replied, pointing to the pistols.

"That's the beauty of it," I returned, dodging the pinch she'd intended for my arm.

"Put 'em back," she said sternly.

"Spoilsport," I grumbled as I obeyed. To my delight, I found something just as noisy and irritating. Rap balls. One push of a button and the round, lighted sphere did a two-minute rap.

"No way!"

"It's my money, I'll spend it the way I want to," I said, moving toward the cashier. I figured it was the least I could do to repay her for calling Dr. Moulton.

"Teri!"

"Too late! I've already paid for them," I said triumphantly, holding up the plastic bag as proof.

"Gee, thanks. Someday I'll return the favor with your kids." As the perfectly normal retort slipped out, my sister flinched, then stiffened. "Teri . . . I . . ."

"It's okay, Deb. It's me, remember. I'm used to this talent you have for wedging your foot in your mouth." I gave her a slight squeeze as we headed out of the store. "And, while we're on the subject, I guess we'd better head back to Dr. Moulton's office. It's almost four o'clock."

Debbie nodded and we left the mall, sobered by thought of what might lie ahead.

This time we took our books from the mall in with us, but we needn't have bothered. For once, as we entered the office, we were taken straight back to Dr. Moulton's private study.

"Must be good news," I quipped nervously. "They've rolled out the red carpet."

"Teri, before he comes in here, I want you to know that I love you and I'm here for you, no matter what we find out."

"I know," I said, avoiding her troubled gaze. Just then, Dr. Moulton entered the room, carrying a rather bulky file. My file. The story of my physical life.

"Good afternoon, ladies," he said, peering over the top of his glasses for a better look at our sweatshirts and shoes. "Nice outfits," he commented. "I guess I didn't notice them earlier."

"Guess not," I said, unwilling to let him off the hook.

He brushed past and sat down behind his desk, setting the file in front of him. "Well, Teri, we did come up with something this afternoon. Where's your husband?"

"Somewhere in Yellowstone Park," I answered.

"I see." He chewed his bottom lip. I glanced at Debbie who was looking as solemn as Dr. Moulton.

"Look, whatever it is, tell me. I can handle it. I'm not pregnant, right? No big deal. I was sure it was the flu, unlike other people I could mention."

"Teri, it's not the flu," Dr. Moulton said quietly. "I'd feel better if Mark was here with you, but he's not and you need to know what's going on."

"Out with it already," I snapped. Then I blushed. I wasn't usually this ornery, at least not in public. Lately, everything seemed to annoy me. "I'm sorry. I didn't mean to be rude, but . . ."

"No need to explain," he said with a smile. "Quite a normal reaction under the circumstances. Teri, you're pregnant."

"See, Deb, I told you . . . WHAT?"

"Oh, Teri," Debbie squealed, rising from her chair to hug me. She practically pulled me off my feet as she yanked me from my chair. "This is so great! Now we'll have babies the same age!" she babbled, pressing me against her. I endured it for a few seconds, then pulled away to glare at my doctor.

"You're kidding?"

"No. There's no doubt about it. And, because of that, there are some things we need to discuss." He gestured to my chair. I sat, but didn't register anything else that was said. I was pregnant? Tears spilled down my face. Suddenly, the small trickle turned into a downpour. Dr. Moulton murmured something about giving us few minutes alone and exited, retreating from a moment I should've been sharing with my husband.

My head whirled when we finally pulled out of the parking lot. For the first time in my life, I was pregnant. Dr. Moulton had confirmed I was nearly six weeks along. I still couldn't believe it. "How is this possible?" I had asked when Dr. Moulton had returned to the room. Grinning at my sister, he had started to explain the facts of life until I cut him off. "I'm serious. We've been careful. Mark has hinted that he'd like to try, but you did say to wait a while before we even considered it. Now what?"

"Well, now we make the best of it and try to keep your blood sugar under control. Your health and your baby's health will depend on it."

I had grimaced, thinking of Sally.

"We'll get through this. One thing I've noticed about you, Teri, you're a fighter. Which is a good thing, because we have quite a battle ahead of us." He had gone on to explain the complications that might occur. Preeclampsia, better known as high blood pressure. Polyhydramnios, a condition that takes place when there is too much amniotic fluid in the sac surrounding the fetus. Macrosomia, which is triggered by high blood glucose levels. The excess sugar crosses the placenta to the fetus, causing the baby to grow too large.

Dr. Moulton had then reassured me that if I could keep my blood sugar levels under tight control, most of these complications could be avoided. "You realize control is critical these first three months? It's important during the rest of the pregnancy, but right now, while your baby is first growing and developing, it's important to keep things on an even keel. It won't be easy, but I know you can do it."

As he continued to discuss the risks involved, I began thinking it was a lost cause until he started the positive approach.

"We want you to know up front what the risks are. It doesn't mean we expect these things to happen, but we want you to be prepared. Now, here's what we want you to do."

Among other things, I learned I would be under the constant supervision of Dr. Moulton and Dr. Setter, a specialist who handles high-risk pregnancies. I was scheduled for an ultrasound on Monday. Mark could come with me and together we would see our baby for the first time. To say I was feeling overwhelmed would have been putting it mildly.

After we left the doctor's office, Debbie correctly sensed that I didn't want to see anyone. She pulled up in front of Edna's house and rounded up her boys as I sat in the car and waited.

That night, Debbie left me home with the boys and braved a sudden storm to pick up a bucket of chicken from the Colonel, and rent a couple of comedies from the video store down the street. When she returned, we ate, put the boys to bed, and watched the videos. Debbie suggested we call our parents, but I refused, wanting Mark to be the next one to know.

When our movie fest ended, we retired upstairs. I didn't feel like being alone, so we had a slumber party of sorts. We settled on sleeping in the guest room and talked long into the night. But, after Debbie started to softly snore on her side of the bed, I found that as tired as I was, I couldn't sleep. I kept imagining this tiny person who was growing inside of me. This infant who would drastically change my life. I tried not to think about Sally as I envisioned what the next few months would bring. Wishing Mark was here to hold me, I silently prayed for my life and the life of my child. A comforting warmth crept into my heart. Clinging to it and my pillow, I slowly drifted off to sleep.

Chapter 16

I had intended for Mark to be the next one to know. And, although I had become quite fond of Edna, if I'd had it my way, she would've been one of the last to learn my news. As fate would have it, she came by the next afternoon to visit and to confirm what the twins had told her the day before.

Debbie and I had purchased unfinished ceramic Valentine decorations earlier that morning and were busy painting them when Edna arrived. We talked Derek into answering the door as we were both engrossed in our artistic project. Derek glanced out the living room window and then eagerly hurried to let Edna in. Chattering nonstop, he led her into the living room to show off the masterpiece he and Eric had created with their new set of Legos. After Edna's assurance that they were indeed genius material, they immersed themselves in building yet another in a series of wondrous edifices. Edna watched for several minutes, then walked into the kitchen. She gazed at the heart-shaped characters on the newspapered counter and sighed heavily to alert us to her presence.

"Your boys remind me so much of Ed and Jake," she said to Debbie. I wondered if my sister felt as insulted as I did. My nephews were nothing like Ed and Jake. And if they ever treated Debbie the way Ed and Jake treated their mother, they'd have me to deal with! "My boys were always building contraptions with their erector sets," Edna continued as she peered over our shoulders. "Aren't those just the cutest things."

"We thought so," Debbie agreed, painting a perfect smile on the ceramic heart she was working on.

I nodded and tried to imitate my sister's skilled ability. The smile I'd painted looked lopsided, but, I decided it added a certain charm.

"Debbie, how are you feeling today?" Edna asked as she eased into a chair near the dining room table. "Your sons mentioned yesterday you'd been sick. That you weren't able to keep your breakfast down. From what they said, I guess it's been happening for quite some time," she said, smiling slyly.

I panicked and wondered what else Debbie's sons had said. It was obvious Edna knew about Debbie's condition. I was sure of it, and prayed she didn't know about mine. Debbie turned to meet Edna's inquisitive gaze. "I feel pretty good today," she said. "I guess the boys told you about the baby?"

Edna nodded. "I think it's wonderful news. I've helped bring enough newborns into this world to know what a miracle it is. Congratulations."

"Thank you," Debbie murmured, her eyes silently communicating with me. The message: calm down. It was only natural Eric and Derek would be anxious to share the news that they were going to be big brothers. It didn't mean they had revealed anything concerning me. I forced a grim smile and tried to relax.

"And I think it's marvelous you two will be having babies together," Edna gushed.

I know my jaw hit the floor. Then I was overcome by a fit of coughing that was so severe, both Debbie and Edna moved to assist. Gradually, I caught my breath. Debbie ran to get a glass of water as Edna firmly steered me toward a dining room chair.

"Take it easy, Teri, breathe deeply," Edna instructed, breathing the way she wanted me to. I ignored her and quickly downed the glass of water. "There now," Edna soothed, "you'll be fine. I hope I didn't say anything to bring this on," she added.

She had, but I decided to let it go. "I didn't know anyone else knew. Mark doesn't even know yet. I just found out yesterday."

"Oh, I'm sorry. Your nephews told me you were going to have a baby, and I figured if they knew, everyone did. That's why I came over, I wanted to congratulate you. I never meant to upset you."

I gave Debbie a dirty look, then glanced at Edna's worried face and softened. I knew she hadn't meant any harm. "It's okay, Edna. I don't mind that you know. But promise me one thing." Edna looked up. "Please don't tell anyone. I want to clue Mark in before anyone else hears, and even then, I'd like to keep it quiet for a while."

"I wish I'd talked to you yesterday," Edna murmured.

I exchanged a look of concern with Debbie. "Tell me no one else knows," I begged.

Edna sank into a chair and looked like she was about to burst into tears. "Teri, I'm sorry. I had no idea . . ." She trailed off sadly.

"How many people know?" I bravely ventured. I felt Debbie's hand grip my shoulder. I wasn't sure if it was to comfort me, or to keep me from tearing Edna apart.

"Not many, and they're so thrilled for you—"

"How many, Edna?" I repeated.

"Well, let's see . . . I mentioned it to my next door neighbor, Florence. She just thought that was the best news she'd heard in a long time. She's going to make you a baby afghan. I told her to pick a neutral color because we don't know if it's a boy or girl yet, do we?" She smiled brightly.

"No, we don't," I answered, grimacing. If Florence Hibbert knew, most of the neighborhood knew. But the damage was done. The milk had been spilled, and it wouldn't do any good to cry over it now, although I suspected throwing a tremendous temper tantrum would make me feel better.

Debbie's grip intensified. She leaned close and whispered, "This too shall pass."

I ignored Deb. "Just Florence, then," I asked hopefully.

Edna slowly shook her head. "I picked up a few groceries later, after you and your sister came to get the boys. I ran into Betty Reeves . . . and Wallace Chattin . . . and, let's see, Mary Duffin . . ." I began to panic; she was using her fingers to count. "Ed Bergen . . ." I flinched. Not Ed. That meant the entire bishopric knew . . . and their wives. "And that cute little Stacie Sayer, you know, Mike and Pam's daughter. She was in the parking lot when I came out of the store. She said 'Hi' and one thing led to another and it slipped out."

I slumped in my chair. Not Stacie Sayer! The teenager thrived on spreading rumors. Natalie had told me she avoided lining Stacie up as a babysitter because of this problem. The girl loved attention and had discovered others were only too willing to listen when dirt was being spread around. The humiliation was complete. I would never be able to show my face in public again. I could imagine the whispers, the smiles, the jokes at my expense. My life was over. I was pregnant and it was sure to be on the six o'clock news. As intense mortification set in, Debbie's grip tightened. "You're married, remember? It's all right for people to know," my sister whispered, somehow guessing my train of thought.

Later, after Edna had apologized for the four hundredth time, she decided to leave. Debbie saw her to the door and assured her everything would be fine. Deb then headed into the kitchen to mix up a couple of mugs of hot chocolate. I was still sitting in shock at the dining room table when she placed a mug in front of me. "It could be worse," she said as she sat down across the table.

"How?" I moaned as I hid my face in my hands.

"Teri, people were going to find out eventually."

I moaned again.

"If it means anything, I felt the same way when I first found out about the twins," she added.

"Really?" I asked, my voice muffled.

"Really. I thought I'd die of embarrassment when word got out. Then I realized something."

"What?"

"People really were happy for me. Having babies is a natural part of life. There's nothing wrong with being pregnant. Especially when you're married to a great guy like Mark."

I slowly lifted my head to gaze at my sister. Encouraged by this, she continued to offer words of wisdom.

"This kind of thing spreads fast anyway. Besides, can you imagine Mark keeping it a secret? He'll be so happy, he'll probably broadcast it all over town."

Edna had already taken care of that, but my sister had a point. Mark would be ecstatic. And, this was something we'd both dreamed about, although it was a dream I'd never thought would come true. Feeling better, I began to sip at my cocoa as Debbie shared pregnancy survival tips, like how to get up from a bench when you're eight months pregnant and the art of rolling out of a water bed. It wasn't long before she had me laughing at her outrageous antics.

"I'll never forget the first time someone asked me if I'd felt life."

"Felt life?"

"That was my question. I had no idea what the woman was talking about. I almost said, 'since the day I was born.' I'm so glad I didn't."

"What did she mean?"

"After a few months, you begin to feel the baby move around."

"Oh," I said, wondering what was in store. "What exactly does that feel like?"

"It depends on how far along you are. At first, kind of like butterflies fluttering around inside. Toward the end, you feel like someone is punting a football against your stomach."

"Serious?"

"Uh huh. Multiply that by two and you have what I endured with Eric and Derek."

"Whoa. Wait a minute. If this is going to turn into one of those horror story sessions, I'm leaving. I don't want to hear how painful or how awful it was. I think it's disgusting when women get together and compare how long they were in labor. It reminds of me of old war veterans who show off their scars, insisting they received them as they performed noble, heroic deeds when in reality a piece of shrapnel hit them while they were in the latrine."

"Teri!"

"I mean it, Deb. I'm scared enough as it is. I don't need to hear any more."

"Look, sis, I'll admit, there are moments that are less than glamorous, but no matter what you have to go through, it's worth it. I'll never regret having children."

"Could I get that in writing?"

Debbie wadded up a napkin and threw it at me. Rising, she set her empty mug on the counter and left the room. I sipped the last of my hot chocolate and pondered her advice. Maybe this wouldn't be so bad. There had been other times in my life when I had needlessly worried about the future. The night of high school graduation. My first week at college. The night I'd accepted Mark's proposal. I'd been so nervous the night before our wedding I hadn't been able to sleep. And look at us now. We'd been married seven years. Seven wonderful years. With any luck, the next seven would be just as wonderful and instead of just the two of us, there would be three, maybe four, if I followed my sister's example. *Whoa!* I thought and nearly jumped out of my chair. Twins did run in our family.

I set my mug in the kitchen sink and went to find Debbie. I had a few more questions to ask. A few more worries to share. And, since everyone else already knew, I'd decided we might as well call Mom and Dad. Mark would understand. Now that it was no longer a secret, I wanted to be the one to tell the news.

Chapter 17

Mark didn't react the way we'd envisioned. He stood with his mouth open, then fainted dead away. Fortunately, Rick was able to grab him before he hit the floor. Debbie ran for a glass of water, but Mark came around before I had the chance to hit him in the face with it. Disappointed, I handed the glass back to my sister.

"You're pregnant?" Mark stammered as he regained his bearings. I nodded. "This is so great!" he exclaimed, sweeping me off my feet in a monstrous hug. "I'm going to be a daddy!" he whooped as he continued to swing me around. Eric and Derek moved out of the way, certain their Uncle Mark had lost his mind. When Mark finally put me down, it was Rick's turn. He gave me a warm embrace and softly kissed my cheek as Mark began to swing my sister around the living room.

"Way to go," Rick whispered in my ear. "I couldn't be happier for you two," he added. Debbie somehow managed to escape Mark and moved to my side for protection.

"Just think, Teri, in a few short months, you and Debbie can compare stretch marks and bask in the glow of motherhood. Isn't it great?" Mark babbled.

"Yeah," I said, wondering if he was serious about the stretch marks. I'd have to ask Debbie about it later. "The best part is that Mom and Dad will be here for this."

"That's right. They'll be home in July. When are we due?" Mark asked.

"We?" I asked.

"Yeah. When are we due?"

Mark was taking his role as daddy very seriously. "August," I answered, trying not to smile.

"Isn't that when you guys are due?" Mark asked Rick.

"Yep," Rick said, enjoying Mark's enthusiasm. "Debbie's supposed to pop this one out around the second week of August."

"Pop this one out?" Debbie said indignantly.

"Is that when our baby gets to come out and play?" Mark asked.

"Pretty close. I'm not due till the end of August, but if they take the baby early . . ."

"Take the baby early?" Mark asked.

"It's a possibility. I might get to go full term, but if we get into trouble, they'd rather take him or her early than risk complications setting in."

"What kind of complications?"

I led Mark to the couch and told him to sit down. Debbie sensed we needed some privacy and shooed her husband and sons into the kitchen.

"What kind of complications?" Mark repeated.

I explained everything Dr. Moulton had told me. When I finished, the color had drained from my husband's face. "It'll be okay, Mark," I said brightly. "You'll see. We'll just have to be careful."

"No kidding," he said quietly.

"It'll be fine," I insisted. "Incidentally, there's one other thing I forgot to add."

"What?" Mark asked somberly.

"The entire state of Idaho already knows."

"What?"

I explained about Edna and managed to get a chuckle out of my husband.

"Leave it to Edna," he said, rising from the couch. "Maybe we ought to have it printed up in the ward bulletin, in case anyone missed the news."

"Not a bad idea," I said, relieved he was lightening up. Mark didn't need to worry himself sick. I was already doing a good enough job for both of us.

That afternoon, Mark decided to give me a blessing. He thought it would make us both feel better. Rick agreed to assist him and decided that while they were at it, they'd give one to Debbie. My sister had told us about the blessing she had received while she was carrying the twins. She felt certain it was responsible for the fairly easy time she'd had during the pregnancy. I hoped for a similar outcome for both of us this time around.

When we explained what we were doing to Eric and Derek, the twins immediately wanted to help. Rick patiently explained they weren't old enough to hold the priesthood, but promised that one day, they could give similar blessings to their own wives. He then told them they could help by being quiet so Heavenly Father could inspire the blessings their mommy and aunt would receive. Eric and Derek solemnly promised to be reverent, and were until Derek decided to bring Bogey into the living room. As Rick firmly escorted Derek and the protesting parrot out of the room, Eric pouted, claiming Bogey's feelings would be hurt. Personally, I didn't care. Bogey and I were already on shaky ground; he was making a mess out of my utility room. Seeds and feathers were everywhere. Not to mention his insistent squawking every time he felt slighted, like now, for instance.

Finally, everyone was ready. Mark and Rick had decided to give Debbie's blessing first. A blessing that was wonderfully inspired. We were all in tears when it was over. Then, it was my turn. I nervously sat in the chair, pondering the promises that had been made to my sister. She would experience good health and have the strength to keep up with her responsibilities as a wife and mother. She had also been promised that this child had a very important purpose here on earth. That purpose was vague, but I wondered if my future niece (I was certain it was going to be a girl) would be burdened with keeping her older brothers in line.

Mark's fingers trembled on my head when it was my turn. The blessing started out as most of them did, with the promise that I would be granted the strength to overcome the trials in my life. Mark's voice cracked. When he continued, an overwhelming spirit of peace and love entered the room. I was told how much my Heavenly Father loved me and that I could call upon Him for the help I would need in the months to come. The tears flowed freely as Mark concluded. Eric wanted to know why we were so sad.

Debbie tried to explain that we were crying happy tears, but I don't think either boy believed her. I heard Derek whisper to his brother that he had never cried happy tears.

The next day, Rick and Debbie packed up to return to Utah. After the car was loaded, Debbie tearfully smiled and reached for a hug. As we drew apart, Derek said disgustedly, "They're crying happy tears again." Debbie guided him back to the car and within minutes, they were on their way to Salt Lake.

Late that night, Natalie and her family returned home. Eager to catch Natalie before Edna did, I showed up on her doorstep about one o'clock the next afternoon.

"Well, hello there," Natalie said, greeting me with a dazzling smile. "It's so good to get home," she added as she hung my coat on a rack near the front door.

"Where is everybody?" I asked, glancing around.

"Our kids were given new sleds for Christmas. They've been dying to try them out. There's not much snow in Pasadena, you know."

"True."

"Jerry took them to the St. Anthony sand dunes for the afternoon. They wanted me to go, but I decided to spend the day attacking the mountain of laundry we brought home."

"Gee, that sounds like fun," I said, relieved she was alone. Not only did I want to share my news, but I was anxious to learn how things had gone in California.

"So, how was Christmas in Idaho Falls?"

"You first. How was California?" I asked as we moved into the living room and sat on the couch.

"Warm. Lots of sun. We came back with tans."

I had already noticed the tan. Natalie looked great. "And?"

"And . . . things went better than I'd thought they would. It wasn't easy. Jerry's mother was really upset at first. She didn't want the past stirred up. But, when she finally understood how tough it had been for Jerry . . . how bad it had gotten between Jerry and me, she quit fighting it. They spent a lot of time talking and working things out. Later on, she went with us to visit the cemetery."

As Natalie continued, I could see that the trip had been a success. Old wounds had been cauterized—wounds that could now begin to heal. Natalie's eyes sparkled with happiness. "I've got my husband back," she said softly. "And I have you to thank for that."

"Not this again," I teased, secretly thrilled that I'd been able to help, even if it was in a small way. "If you don't quit giving me so much credit, I'll end up with an ego the size of Mark's."

"I doubt that. Not that Mark has an ego problem," she hastily added. "Anyway, I'm dying to know. How did it go with Edna?"

"Let me start by saying you were correct in your assumption that there is more to our secretary than meets the eye."

"Serious?"

Nodding, I told her what had taken place Christmas Day.

"I can't believe those sons of hers. Why didn't they call?"

"I don't know. If I were Edna, I'd put them up for adoption."

"Well, I'm glad you and Mark invited her over. It sounds like she enjoyed herself."

"She did. And we enjoyed having her there."

"I'm glad. I have to admit, I was a little worried."

"I'm hurt."

Natalie smiled. "You know what I mean. I wanted Christmas to be wonderful for everyone. That included you. I knew you weren't overly thrilled about having Edna as a guest."

"Yeah, well, it turned out fine. At least, the Christmas part of it."

"Did something else happen?"

"As a matter of fact," I began. Just then, the phone rang.

"Hold that thought," Natalie said as she hurried out of the living room to answer. Although she was enjoying a day on her own, I could tell she was worried about her family. She'd already mentioned several times that she hoped everyone would return home in one piece. I knew she was afraid the phone call meant someone had been hurt.

While I waited, I wandered over to the piano to look at the pictures displayed on top. I gazed at a baby picture of Kimberly and tried to imagine how I'd tell Natalie about my baby. I could hardly wait, even though I knew what was in store for me—another one of her infamous hugs.

Suddenly, Natalie squealed. Before I could rush into the kitchen to see what was wrong, she came racing into the living room and nearly knocked the wind out of me as she drew me into an embrace.

"Oh, Teri, this is so neat! When did you find out? Why didn't you say anything?"

"What are you talking about?" I gasped.

Natalie drew back to give me an extremely dirty look. "Why am I the last to know?"

"Was that Edna on the phone?" I asked, certain of what had happened.

"No, it was Gloria. She wanted to know if I'd conduct for her this Sunday. She and Ian have been invited to her parents' house in Ogden for the weekend." Natalie folded her arms and continued to glare. "She also wanted to know if I'd heard you were pregnant. Why didn't you tell me?"

"I was about to. Honest. That's why I came over. I wanted to tell at least one person. Edna's taken care of everyone else. She ought to go to work for the *Post Register*. She gets the news out faster than anyone I know."

Natalie laughed, gave me another hug, then led me back to the couch to pump me for details. She enjoyed the part about my thinking it was the flu. "You know, I was starting to wonder. The week before Christmas, you didn't look so hot. You had the same greenish tint as Gloria."

"I did not."

"You did, trust me. Wow. I can't believe both of my counselors are pregnant."

"Don't worry, we'll still be able to . . ."

"I'm not worried about that. I'm afraid I'll get so baby hungry I'll end up in a similar condition."

"Would that be all bad?"

"No. Jerry's hinted for months he'd like to add to our collection of offspring."

"Well then?"

"I want to give him more time before we bring another child into this family. He's had a lot to deal with lately . . . we both have."

"True," I sighed. I glanced at my watch, surprised that so much time had passed. "Guess I'd better hurry home and get dinner started. See you later."

"Okay. In the meantime, take it easy."

"Don't worry, it's what I do best," I said as I stepped out onto the porch.

I was still trying to decide what to make out of the leftovers in the fridge when Mark came through the door. He walked into the kitchen, passionately kissed me, and then suggested we dress up and hit a fancy restaurant.

"We've celebrated our news with everyone else. Tonight, I want you all to myself," he said as he nibbled on my ear. Who was I to argue with that kind of logic? Shutting the fridge, I followed Mark upstairs to change.

Chapter 18

Just like Deb had said, people were happy for Mark and me. Everywhere we went, we were congratulated, offered advice, and promised that this would be the happiest time of our lives. I believed them. I couldn't remember ever being this elated, with the exception of the night Mark had proposed. And now, our love had produced a child.

Mark took the day off to go with me to my first appointment with Dr. Setter. He was younger than Dr. Moulton, but seemed competent. He laughed easily, a trait that I consider important. I like a doctor with a sense of humor. Humor often eases the tension that can occur in a doctor/patient relationship.

I nearly jumped out of my skin when Gina, Dr. Setter's assistant, lifted up the flimsy gown to rub a gooey substance on my stomach in preparation for the ultrasound. Her hands felt like she'd just finished examining an iceberg. Later Dr. Setter came into the examining room and began to educate us concerning our baby.

"That's the what?" Mark asked again, staring at the fuzzy image on the screen.

"Your baby's temporary home. And this tiny guy is the reason you came to see me," he added, pointing to a blurred section.

"She's a boy?" I asked, disappointed. I had hoped to have a girl, a playmate for Debbie's future daughter.

"Don't know yet. I trade genders weekly. This week, everyone's a boy. Next week, they're all girls. I like to keep my patients guessing."

"Can you ever tell from the ultrasound whether they're boys or girls," Mark asked.

"Sometimes. Sometimes these little tykes are shy and refuse to expose themselves. Even when they do, I rarely share that knowledge unless the parents insist. I think it takes the fun out of it." He smiled and began to scrutinize the image on the screen. I had been instructed to lie still and was doing my best to comply. Then, suddenly, I sneezed.

"Oh, no," Dr. Setter exclaimed.

"What?" I asked panicking.

"Junior's missing."

Mark quickly stood and stared at the screen, a horrified expression on his face. Dr. Setter looked at Mark, then laughed so hard, we knew he wasn't serious.

"Not funny," I retorted.

"Sorry, I couldn't resist. I love first-time parents. You're so fun to tease."

Mark looked like he wanted to punch the doctor, but I made him sit down and behave. If this was the guy who was going to pull us through, we had better stay on good terms with him. Besides, Dr. Moulton wasn't easily impressed; he must have his reasons for sending us to him.

"Things look okay so far. Let me get a few measurements, then we'll let you get dressed, Teri." Dr. Setter had correctly guessed we'd had enough merriment for one day and adopted a businesslike attitude. "Hmmmmm."

"What?" Mark asked, panicking again.

"Oh, it's probably nothing."

"Feel free to share it with us," I encouraged.

"Well, Junior isn't quite as big as he should be, if we've figured the date of conception correctly."

I tried not to blush, but failed.

"Our baby isn't big enough?" Mark stammered.

"Oh, he's probably fine. We must have miscalculated somewhere." Dr. Setter reached for my chart and made a few notes. "I see we were anticipating an August delivery date."

"Yes," I answered.

"So, that would put us about six weeks along now, correct?"

"Yes," I repeated.

"Okay. According to the readings I'm getting today, I'm wondering if we're off a couple of weeks. Is that a possibility?"

"I suppose," I murmured.

"That's got to be our answer then," he said brightly, concentrating again on the blur that was supposedly our baby. He took a few more measurements, asked a few more questions, and then was gone, onto the next patient who was waiting for him in a room just like this one down the hall. After I dressed, Gina led me back to the receptionist's desk to set up another appointment.

"Dr. Setter wants to see you in one week for another ultrasound," Gina said brightly. As the receptionist logged the appointment on the computer, Gina rummaged around in a cupboard behind the desk. Finally, she emerged bearing a small plastic container and handed it to me with a smile. "You'll need to bring a sample with you every time you come," she explained.

"Oh," I said, my face burning again. I quickly tucked the offending bottle into my purse and ignored the grin on Mark's face.

"Gee, that was fun," he said later as we pulled out of the parking lot.

"Yeah. I live for these moments," I replied.

"Did you see the rather large lady who rolled into the office before we went back to meet with Dr. Setter?"

"Uh huh," I said, recalling the short pregnant woman who had been nearly as round as she was tall. I smiled, then frowned. "Is that how I'm going to look?"

"No. But, if you put on a few pounds, it'll just mean there's more of you to love."

"I feel so much better now, Mark."

"Good," he said brightly. "Now, in honor of our child's first Kodak moment, let's go out to lunch."

"Cathay's? I love their buffet."

"Chinese cuisine it is," he agreed. As he drove toward the restaurant, I gazed at the picture printout of our baby and caressed the shadowed image. We'd been promised a videotape of Junior next week. I could hardly wait.

Debbie called me later that night. "So, how did the ultrasound go?"

"Fine, but it sounds like I may not be due in August."

"Oh?"

"Yeah. Our baby's not as big as he's supposed to be."

"He?"

"That's what Dr. Setter called him. He doesn't know for sure, next week it'll be a she. He likes to keep us guessing."

"Sounds like a fun guy," Debbie murmured. "Does he know his stuff?"

"He must if Dr. Moulton suggested him."

"So, when are you due?"

"The second week of September. It depends on how things go. If they take the baby the last of August, we'll still have our babies the same month."

"That would be neat, but the most important thing is . . ."

"I know. I know. Don't worry, Junior and I will be fine."

"I can't help worrying. Remember what Mom said, I'm supposed to keep track of you while she's gone."

"I'm a big girl, Deb."

"Soon to be bigger."

"Not funny!"

"I know. Sorry."

"Rick's rubbing off on you," I muttered.

"Now it's your turn to apologize," my sister demanded. We talked and laughed for nearly thirty minutes until our respective husbands both began to give us grief concerning the expense of the call. "Guess I'd better go," Debbie sighed. "Take it easy and call if you need anything."

"If Mark lets me near the phone again," I replied. "Thanks for keeping in touch."

"Get used to it," Debbie assured me. "Let me know how the next appointment goes."

"Okay." We bid each other adieu and I allowed Mark to guide me into the living room for a foot massage. He soon had me so relaxed I fell asleep, which wasn't exactly what he had in mind. But, being the good sport that he is, he gently led me upstairs to get ready for bed.

Chapter 19

The following Sunday, I nudged Mark when Emmett Hunt walked into the chapel. We hadn't seen him since Christmas Eve. He marched up the aisle, scowling at everyone in his path. Unfortunately, Bishop Anderson had picked that moment to congratulate us again on our "news" and to find out how my appointment had gone. When Emmett spotted the bishop, he seemed to get a gleam in his eye. Pushing a teenage boy out of his way, Emmett bore down on us.

"Bishop, we need to talk!" Emmett snarled.

"Why, Brother Hunt, it's good to see you," the bishop replied.

"Don't give me that," Emmett said angrily. "When are you gonna come pick up that welfare box you dumped off on my porch?"

"Now, Emmett—" Bishop Anderson began.

"Don't you Emmett me! You had no business traipsin' by with that lot of do-gooders, trespassin' on my land, stirrin' up trouble!"

The bishop opened his mouth to offer a rebuttal, but, just then, Edna came on the scene. "Brother Hunt, you ought to be ashamed of yourself!" she said firmly. "Speaking like that to our good bishop."

"I'll speak the way I please! Especially when it's to the no-good, low-down varmint who leaves a charity box on my doorstep Christmas Eve!"

"He was only trying to help you have a merry Christmas," Edna replied. "And this is how you show gratitude? I think you have some apologizing to do!"

Mark and I exchanged a concerned look; Edna could be as stubborn as Emmett could ever hope to be.

"Look, woman—"

"Sister Barrett," Edna said sternly.

"Whatever you call yourself. This is none of your affair. I suggest you move on and poke your nose elsewhere!"

Edna frowned. "Brother Hunt, your manners are atrocious!" she said. "That is no way to speak to a lady!"

"Who said you were a lady?"

Edna began to swing her Primary bag in a dangerous fashion. The bishop gave us a pleading look for help as he attempted to steer Emmett out into the hall. Mark and I tried to calm Edna down, but it was clear she had been deeply offended.

"That man . . ." she sputtered. "That . . . horrible man!"

"It's just Emmett," I soothed as we tried to get her to sit down. It was nearly time for sacrament meeting to begin.

"I'll be right back," Edna promised. We helplessly followed her out into the hall. "Emmett Hunt," she thundered.

Emmett turned from where he was lecturing the bishop to glare at Edna.

"YOU are no gentleman!" Then, having had the last word, Edna whirled around and stomped back inside of the chapel.

Emmett looked surprised and rubbed at his chin. "Spunky busybody," he muttered.

We'd left Hank Clawson sitting by himself in the chapel and as the opening hymn began, hurried to his side. Edna had elected to sit by Gloria and Ian in the bench across from ours. We smiled at her, but she kept her focus straight ahead.

After the opening prayer, Sylvia Clawson slipped into the meeting. Mark had leaned back to stretch and spotted her. Pleasantly surprised, he pointed her out to me. She was wearing the sweater we'd given her with a nice skirt, her hair done up in a chignon. She looked very nice, but ill at ease. I finally caught her attention and we slid down the bench so she could sit by her son.

The meeting was wonderful. The speakers were an older couple from our ward who had been asked to talk about setting goals. Sister Evans humorously touched on the tradition of making half-hearted New Year resolutions that are usually forgotten or broken during the year. Her advice was to select only one or two goals to avoid feeling overwhelmed, and gradually work on improving ourselves. A musical number was then rendered by the choir, of which I am a semi-faithful member. Following it, Brother Evans picked up where his wife left off and tied setting goals with the importance of living gospel principles. He promised that if we'd use the same strategy mentioned by his wife, we could overcome weaknesses and strengthen our testimonies as we reach toward eternal happiness.

Sylvia Clawson looked lost in thought at the close of the meeting. As we moved out into the foyer, she grabbed my arm and steered me into a corner. "I don't think I've ever thanked you for bringing Hank to church," she said quietly.

"We've enjoyed doing it," I replied.

"I really have appreciated what you and your husband have done for my son, but—"

"He's never been a problem."

"What I'm trying to say is that Hank won't need a ride anymore."

I blinked. Was something wrong? Had something or someone insulted her? Had she resented the remarks made today during Sacrament Meeting?

"I'll bring him myself—when I can come," Sylvia said with a smile. "On the Sundays that I have to work, I'll make arrangements for him to be here."

"Mark and I would be happy to pick him up when you have to work," I said, overjoyed.

"You've already done so much . . ."

"We'd consider it a privilege. We've grown quite fond of Hank."

"I know he adores both of you. All right. If you're sure it's not too much trouble."

"Positive."

She smiled, then walked away to find her son. As for me, I hurried off to find Mark. I could hardly wait to tell him what Sylvia had said.

Sylvia wasn't the only one who began coming out to church on a regular basis. Emmett Hunt's attendance record also improved. At first, I wondered if he'd taken Brother Evan's challenge seriously. Then I started catching on. He stayed out in the hall until Edna came into view and made it a point to confront her. Sometimes heated words were exchanged, sometimes glares, but always, Emmett walked away grinning. I knew what it was; Emmett had finally found a worthy opponent. I took secret delight in Edna's quick-witted comebacks and hoped she could continue to put the old rascal in his place.

I wasn't the only one who had observed this strange relationship. One warm afternoon the first week of March, Natalie, Gloria and I decided to go for a "mug run" and refill our drinks after our presidency meeting. Edna declined, claiming she had errands to attend to.

"Have you noticed how Emmett Hunt always picks a fight with Edna whenever he sees her?" Natalie asked as we buckled into her car.

"I think the entire ward has noticed," Gloria said with a grin.

"What do you think is going on?"

Now it was my turn to smile at Natalie. "Emmett's finally met his match and it serves him right. He'll never out-argue Edna."

"I think he likes her," Gloria said, a mischievous twinkle in her eye.

"What? That old coot? No way!" I exclaimed.

"Stranger things have happened," Natalie said, smiling brightly. "They are about the same age, you know."

"You guys are disgusting," I returned. "The thought of those two together is disgusting. The thought of Emmett Hunt alone is disgusting enough, but Edna and Emmett? C'mon, that's like pairing up two heavy-weight champions. They'd kill each other."

"Where's your sense of romance, Teri?" Gloria asked.

"I can be as romantic as anybody else . . ."

"I know," Natalie teased. "So does the entire ward," she added as she pulled into the Maverik parking lot.

"Quit interrupting. I'm being serious here. Emmett and Edna are nothing more than sparring partners. Emmett takes great delight in antagonizing Edna every chance he gets. That's not love, that's spite. Besides," I said, shuddering, "Edna deserves better than Emmett Hunt."

"Now, now . . . when he cleans up, Emmett doesn't look too bad. Haven't you noticed that he smells better these days?" Natalie asked.

"No, but then, I don't normally go around sniffing the men in our ward," I said impishly.

"Neither do I," Natalie said dryly as Gloria started to giggle. Ignoring us, Natalie climbed out of the car.

"There have been times when we've all tried to stay upwind of Emmett," Gloria contributed, trying to keep a straight face.

"True," I agreed as we walked down the sidewalk. "Which is another reason Edna won't have anything to do with him. She'd start every date dousing him in Lysol."

"You're probably right," Natalie sighed as she held the door open. "But, I hate to see Edna spend the rest of her life alone," she said as we moved into the convenience store.

"Trust me, she'd be better off on her own than with that degenerate," I said firmly. "Anyway, Edna can't stand the man. Yesterday during Primary, she was muttering under her breath. I thought one of the Hale twins had set her off again."

"And?" Natalie asked.

"And, when I asked her what was wrong, she informed me Emmett Hunt was a carbuncle on society's behind." At this Natalie rolled her eyes and began to fill her mug.

"Emmett has about as much chance of winning Edna as Mark has naming our baby Bosephus." I insisted. "Trust me, I know these things."

"Bosephus?" Gloria asked, then sipped her newly replenished mug.

"He was trying to be funny and didn't succeed."

"I'll say. That's pretty bad." Gloria gave me a funny look as I reached for a bottle of V-8. I'd sworn off pop since I'd learned about Junior.

"You're pretty sure about Emmett and Edna, aren't you," Natalie stated.

"Positive," I returned. "Emmett doesn't stand a snowball's

chance in . . . how shall I put this delicately?"

"Florida?" Gloria offered.

I nodded and moved to the counter to pay for our drinks. Natalie argued with me until I pointed out that she had paid the last time we'd come.

"My turn next time," Gloria offered.

"How about a little side bet?" Natalie asked as we moved out of the store.

"You want to make a bet out of this?" Gloria asked, intrigued.

"Uh huh. Who among us thinks love is in the air? Bear in mind we're discussing this in terms of Edna and Emmett." Natalie gazed at both of us.

"I'd say it's possible," Gloria said blithely.

"I can't believe you two," I said, shaking my head.

"Are we to assume that's a 'No'?"

I gave Natalie an incredulous look and nodded.

"Okay. Two of us say 'yes', and one very stubborn individual is sticking to 'no'. Let's say if Teri's right, and nothing of a romantic nature happens with these two in the next six months, we'll clean her house for a week."

"Gee, that sounds like fun," Gloria groaned.

"You'll be doing my fall cleaning. I like it," I said brightly.

"If we're right, and something develops, Teri will handle a couple of our Sharing Times," Natalie continued.

"Now, wait just a minute. I would do two Sharing Times for each of you?" I asked.

"Uh huh. Deal?" Natalie pressed, a wicked gleam in her eye.

"And you're only cleaning my house for a week?"

"I saw the shape your house was in today. I think the bet's fair," Gloria said in our leader's defense.

"You're a riot," I retorted as I slid into Nat's car.

"Do we have a deal?" Natalie held out her hand.

"Okay," I said, shaking first her extended hand, then reaching back to shake Gloria's. Certain of my victory, I drank a toast to myself. "Here's to the cleanest shine my house will ever endure," I said, ignoring the look on Natalie's face.

Later, after she dropped me off at my somewhat cluttered

abode, I decided it could do with some sprucing up. After all, it would be six months before Natalie and Gloria arrived to make it smell like Lemon Pledge.

By the time Mark came home from work, the place looked great. Stunned, my smart-aleck husband went back outside to gaze at the numbers on the front of our house to make sure he had the right address. I got even during supper. When he wasn't looking, I doused his enchilada with a generous helping of Tabasco sauce.

Chapter 20

The next morning, it was obvious my body was intent on rebelling. Closing my eyes against the nausea, I stayed in bed long after Mark got up. I assured my worried husband I would be fine, convinced it was paybacks from the Mexican food we'd consumed the night before. He made me promise to call if I started feeling worse and reluctantly left for work.

After I finally pulled myself out of bed, I experimented with several home remedies for morning sickness, but despite the crackers, toast, and tea, my stomach wouldn't let up. I spent most of the morning in the bathroom before deciding to get hold of Dr. Setter. It was probably nothing, but, I wanted to check with him to make sure.

I had started downstairs to call when the cramping started. I clutched at the wooden railing and leaned against it, holding my breath. When it wouldn't let up, I knew I was in trouble. I made it down the rest of the stairs, but my head was spinning as I stumbled into the dining room. Another pain hit, one so intense it took my breath away. It was followed by another. I reached for the table, stumbled, hit my head and pitched forward as everything went black.

"Teri! C'mon, don't do this to me . . . please be all right! Teri?" Natalie pleaded.

I opened my eyes, but couldn't focus. Another cramp hit, causing me to moan.

"Teri? Can you hear me?"

I tried to nod.

"Where's your monitor? Is it your blood sugar? How long have you . . . oh, no! Where is that ambulance?!" Natalie shifted my head from her lap to the floor and ran out of the room. When she came back, it looked like she had gathered a fist full of rags or towels. I tried to speak, but another cramp hit. I tried to cry out, but the only audible sound was a siren.

Chapter 21

It was a week of confusion and pain. I spent a day and a half in the hospital, then Mark brought me home. Debbie came to stay and did her best to make things easier for me. I was too numb to respond, but she kept trying, as did Mark, Natalie, and an endless parade of others. They came, offering comfort and advice. But, as hard as they tried, no one could explain, and no one answered the questions I couldn't ask. I pushed the pain down deep and kept to myself as much as possible, staring for endless hours, seeing only the child that might have been.

"Teri?"

It was Debbie again.

"I fixed waffles this morning. Why don't you come down and eat? You've been cooped up in this room for days. I think the change would do you some good."

I didn't want to change. I would stay in my room forever. *Maybe if I ignore her, she'll go away,* I thought as I continued to stare out the bedroom window.

"It'll get easier," Debbie said softly. She moved behind my chair and put her arms around my shoulders. "I know you're hurting. I wish—"

I didn't want to hear what she was saying so I pulled from her, moved into the bathroom, and closed the door.

"Teri, come out of there," Debbie demanded. "Mark told me before he left for work that you've already given your shot. You need to eat or you'll go on your head."

Wearily I leaned against the sink, turned on the water, and

watched as it poured down the drain.

Debbie tried the door, but I had locked it. "Teri, this is ridiculous. Open this door." I heard her try the knob again. "I know what you're doing. I've seen this before, remember? When we found out about the diabetes. You kept a wall between yourself and everyone else. You told us we didn't understand. Maybe we didn't, but do you know how many nights I cried myself to sleep wishing I could change it for you? How helpless I felt because I couldn't do anything about it? Every day, I wondered why it was you and not me."

I'd asked that question myself. Only I hadn't been as selfless as my sister.

"Teri, I'd give anything if I could make this one go away. I can't . . . no one can. The only thing I can offer is love . . . and you'll always have that."

Her sincerity made it difficult to be resentful. Difficult, but not impossible. Her baby was fine. She'd probably have twelve kids without any problem. Things always worked out for Debbie. Always.

I tried to shut out her voice as she said, "If you'd just let it out . . . I don't think you've cried once since you came home from the hospital. You can't keep it inside and you can't do it alone. Now, open this door."

Several minutes passed before she finally gave up. I knew she would. Eventually, everyone would. I shut off the water. My hands were shaking. Debbie was right, I was headed for a major reaction. The trouble was, I didn't care.

A strange scratching sound startled me. Turning, I saw that a Hershey's chocolate bar had been stuffed under the door.

"Eat!" Debbie said sternly. "I'll give you two minutes to wolf it down. If, in that amount of time, you can't prove to me that you've eaten it, I will break this door down. That is a promise. Then, you'll be one sorry young lady!"

It was so bizarre, I almost laughed out loud. It was a scene from our teens. I'd had a major fight with our parents after cheating on my diet. My parents had approached me before supper that night. Following the stern lecture, I was on a real self-pity kick. I'd already given a shot of insulin, but instead of sitting down to eat with the rest of the family, I'd locked myself in the bathroom. In retaliation, Dad had angrily shoved candy under the door, using the same threat Debbie had used.

"Teri!"

I was tired of this battle. "Leave me alone!" I said angrily.

"You've wasted one minute already. I suggest you get eating!"

I didn't want to give in, but knew if I didn't, I would pass out in a very short time. Then, Debbie could take revenge by driving me back to the hospital. I had no wish to return to that prison. Angrily, I tore open the candy bar and began stuffing the chocolate in my mouth. As she started the final countdown, I shoved the empty wrapper under the door.

"How do I know you didn't unwrap the candy bar and throw it away?"

I didn't want to open the door as I had done for Dad. I didn't want to see the pain in her eyes. So I deliberately forced a loud belch. "There!"

"You're disgusting, do you know that?" Debbie exclaimed.

I don't care, I told myself. *I don't care about a lot of things, actually. Maybe in time, people will catch on.*

That afternoon, Debbie took the twins and went grocery shopping. In her absence, I wandered listlessly around the house. The phone rang several times, but I let it ring. The doorbell intruded, but I ignored it. Evidently, my sister had forgotten to lock the door because a few minutes later, Edna marched into where I was sitting in the living room.

"I guess you didn't hear the bell," she said, fixing me with a piercing gaze.

"Guess not," I murmured, surprised by her intensity.

She sat beside me on the couch. "I came by while you were in the hospital, but you were sleeping. Then I stopped for a visit two days ago, but Debbie said you weren't up to company." Her face seemed to soften for a moment, but I didn't encourage her by making small talk. The silent treatment had worked to get rid of other unwanted guests; it would work on Edna.

It didn't stop her, although her voice was more quiet than I'd ever known Edna to be as she said, "You know, dear, there are times when we all feel . . . challenged—when we feel that life is . . . unfair."

I closed my eyes and sighed. The last thing I needed was a pep talk. Standing up, I pulled my robe around me and began to walk out of the room.

"Teri, you're stronger than this." Now she sounded like the same old Edna. Enraged, I turned to face her, but she spoke before I could open my mouth.

"True, you're going through a rough time. When I worked as a nurse, I saw more than my share of miscarriages. I have yet to see a woman who isn't devastated when it happens. It's only right that you take some time to grieve. Just remember, others are grieving with you. You're not alone in this."

I made the unfortunate mistake of rolling my eyes. "Teri," she said, exasperated. "Quit tuning us out! Do you have any idea how you're hurting everyone around you?"

"I haven't hurt anyone," I said stubbornly. "I just don't want to talk right now. No one understands what I'm feeling—"

"That's where you're wrong, missy!" It was evident that Edna was ticked. But then, so was I. I opened my mouth to defend myself, but Edna bulldozed right over me.

"They love you, but you're too blind to see it! I stopped at Natalie's house yesterday with an attendance report she had to sign. I could tell she'd been crying. When I asked what was wrong, she said she'd been over to see you. She said you wouldn't even talk to her."

I felt a twinge of guilt but ignored it. "I didn't have anything to say," I said shortly.

"I think it's high time you realize what you're doing to yourself and everyone else!"

And she thought she was here to help me? Right!

She continued. "The other day when I came by to see you, Debbie looked like she'd been through a war. She's worried sick about you, which isn't good, considering her condition."

"Oh, she's fine!" I hissed sarcastically. She was pregnant and healthy.

"And how would you know? Have you asked her?" Edna snapped.

"As for your husband, someone who is hurting as much as you are, I might add—he adores you. You're lucky to have someone like him in your life. Not many men would be as understanding with your chronic health problem as—"

"Oh, you mean I should count my blessings that Mark took pity and married a diabetic!"

"Of course not. It's obvious that man would love you if you had leprosy. I've worked with several diabetics and their spouses. Compared to some of them, Mark is a real gem. He worries over you, treats you like a queen, and right now, would do anything to take away this pain you're feeling."

"Edna, you better leave now before I say something I'll regret," I warned.

"Not until you make me a promise."

I just stared at her. I couldn't believe the nerve of this woman.

"Teri," she said softly, "quit acting like me."

That was it! I'd had enough! The camel's back was broken and it wasn't by a straw! I was too angry to talk. Clenching my fists, I moved out of the room. Edna followed me into the kitchen.

"I don't know if Mark ever told you, but my husband, Charlie, was killed in an accident nearly thirty-five years ago. He worked for the railroad. He was caught between two freight cars that had come unfastened. He was realigning the couplers when the car behind him slid forward."

I closed my eyes to block out the mental picture she'd forced upon me. It wasn't pleasant.

"That left me alone to raise our two sons—two boys who were hurting over losing their father. But I was so consumed with my own angry pain, I didn't understand what they were going through. Instead, I increased my hours at the hospital to keep busy. As a result, I wasn't around much when Ed and Jake needed me.

"Edna—" I began.

"Settle down, I'm not finished! After Charlie's death, I didn't want to leave myself open to that kind of pain again. I had to be in control of everyone . . . of every situation. In the process, I drove a permanent wedge between myself and my sons, not to mention those friends who had tried to stand by me. And now, I'm alone. There are no friends to lean on. My sons never call or write. I haven't seen them in years. My bitterness pushed everyone away."

I didn't look at her. "So why are you telling me this?"

"Because you're starting down a similar path, and I care too much to watch that happen." When I finally looked up at her, she held my gaze for several seconds, before she walked out of the kitchen.

"I'm not like you," I sputtered, following behind her. "Not like you at all!"

"Think about what I said," Edna as she headed out the front door. "Think about it long and hard."

When she left, I picked up a book and hurled it at the door. I was about to storm upstairs when the phone rang. Whirling around, I marched into the kitchen and shut it off. Then, I moved down the hall into the study to shut that phone off as well. That left the bedroom line. As I headed upstairs, the doorbell rang.

"Great! It's probably Natalie, A.K.A. Mary Poppins, or the well-intentioned Gloria, or maybe even the famed Bishop Anderson! Maybe Edna has returned for round two. Well, I've got news for all of them! I'm finished! Through! They can take this Church calling and . . ." I fumed as I stomped toward the door. I flung it open, glaring at the would-be intruder. It was Hank.

"I . . . I missed you at . . . at Primary yesterday," he stuttered.

I continued to glare. Natalie had probably sent him over, thinking I would soften. Well, she was wrong!

"We watched a . . . a Book of Mormon video in Sharing Time," he added, offering a shy smile. "It was neat. Will you come . . . next Sunday?"

Something in me snapped. "No, I won't come next week or the week after that! Now, leave me alone! All of you just leave me alone!"

A horrified look spread across his face. Turning, he fled. Guilt intensified the pain in my heart.

I hurried after him, calling his name. "Hank, wait, I didn't mean it. Hank, wait up!" He continued to run, lifting a hand to wipe at his eyes. Cursing under my breath, I followed. "Hank, come back here!" I panted. I couldn't keep up. My head whirled. Fighting the dizziness, I paused to catch my breath, then continued the chase. "HANK," I hollered loudly. He looked over his shoulder, but didn't stop. Just then, I slipped on a patch of ice. I tried to regain my balance, but failed and came down hard on the sidewalk, my right arm twisting behind me. It began to throb sharply.

"Are you okay?"

I gazed up into Hank's concerned face. "No, Hank, I'm not okay," I answered, thinking a broken arm would serve me right. I tried to apologize as he helped me to my feet. "I'm sorry, Hank. I didn't mean to yell at you."

"It's okay," he said with a small smile. "You're sick. My mom gets mad when she doesn't feel good too." Then, acting as though he didn't need any other explanation, he guided me down the sidewalk toward my house.

Once inside, Hank helped me into a chair and called Mark at the computer store. While he was on the phone with my husband, my sister pulled up. I took the phone from Hank and told Mark we'd meet him at the hospital.

As Debbie made her way to the house with her sons and two sacks of groceries, Hank filled her in on what had taken place. She refrained from passing judgement on my behavior, focusing instead on my injury. Quickly filling an ice pack, she wrapped it in a towel and placed it against my arm. She then managed to locate the Tylenol in the cluttered cupboard above the fridge. We ran a quick check on my blood sugar—pain always drops my level. It was a low 57. After Debbie helped me drink a glass of apple juice, she and Hank guided me out of the house and into her car.

Hank sat next to me in the back seat, his hand protectively enfolding mine. "You'll be okay," he assured me. I nodded, wishing I had his faith.

The x-rays confirmed what I already knew, the arm was fractured. My husband and sister anxiously paced the hall floor as the doctor on call and an efficient nurse patched me back together. Hank had helped me select fluorescent pink for my cast. And, after it was officially in place, I let him have the honor of being the first to sign it. With a fine-point black marker he wrote:

> To my best friend in Primary,
> Love, Hank

Mark then took the marker and scribbled his message:

> To my favorite spouse,
> Hugs & Kisses, Mark

Debbie helped her sons write their names, then inscribed:

> To the best sister in the world.
> Love ya, Deb

I knew there wasn't a word of truth to what she'd written. Debbie had already earned that title.

Chapter 22

The days that followed were difficult. Being right-handed didn't help matters. I'm a prideful person and with my right arm in a cast, I was terribly dependent on others. Mark and Debbie didn't seem to mind as much as I did. Neither had said a word about how I'd managed to fall, even though Hank had shared the details with both of them. Instead, they tried to make the best of it, never hinting that I'd brought it on myself. They took turns giving my insulin shots and assisting me with my blood sugar checks. One or the other had to help me in and out of the tub when I took a bath, and getting dressed was another adventure in humiliation.

The shock of how I'd treated Hank kept me pretty humble. I vowed I wouldn't let myself get that far out of control again. When Natalie came by to visit and sign my cast, I smiled and tried to be pleasant, steering clear of anything too serious. There was a hurt look in her eye when she left, but I couldn't help it. I wasn't ready to expose the pain in my heart.

Bishop Anderson and his wife came to see me the day after I broke my arm. I visited with them for a several minutes, then asked to speak to the bishop alone. I think he was afraid I was going to ask to be released, but I surprised him. I merely wanted some questions answered. He later said the release might've been easier.

"So, what's on your mind?" he asked, sitting in the chair next to my bed.

"Do you remember the blessing I was given by Ed . . . Brother Ed Bergen?"

"When we set you apart?"

I nodded. "He said there would be children coming into our home."

"I figured we would be having this conversation sooner or later. Teri, I'll be honest. I was concerned that night. I knew how sensitive that issue was, and when I asked Ed about it later, he mentioned he was worried too. But he also said he couldn't ignore the prompting that came. If you'll remember, the Spirit was very strong that night. Ed was inspired to say what he did."

"Then why . . ."

"We have no way of knowing when certain events are to take place in our lives or how those events will transpire. But, the power of the priesthood is real, and one way or another, you'll see that promise fulfilled."

I shuddered as a shiver raced along my spine. Ignoring the sensation, I hit him with my next question. "There's something else I don't understand. In December, when we first found out about our baby, Mark and my brother-in-law gave me a blessing. I had the best feeling inside; I was positive everything would be fine."

"Were you promised this baby would be born healthy and strong?"

I reflected on what had been said. "No, not in so many words, but I assumed she . . ." I faltered, thinking of my tiny daughter. Junior had been a girl.

"Sometimes we misinterpret blessings. Mark spoke to me a few days ago. He had some concerns about the blessing too. As we talked, he said that while his hands were on your head, he sensed a great trial was in store . . . for both of you. At the time, he thought it would be the pregnancy."

"You're saying it was the miscarriage?"

"Maybe."

"I was so sure it would work out. I mean, I was scared at first, especially when Dr. Moulton told me about the risks involved. But, after the blessing, I thought we'd be okay. I can't believe Heavenly Father let us down like this."

"Teri—"

"I know. You're going to say I'm wrong to feel this way, right?"

"Actually, I was going to say that what you're feeling is perfectly normal under the circumstances. There are times when we feel alone . . . when we think we've been deserted or abandoned. What we fail to realize is that those are the times we're carried."

"I don't feel like I'm being carried," I sniffed, looking away.

"Mark said you've refused a priesthood blessing since the miscarriage. What would you think about having one now?"

I remained silent. Part of me longed for spiritual assurance, but another portion of my heart blamed God for ignoring my prayers.

"I think it would help," the bishop said, rising from the chair. "But, that's something only you can decide."

"Maybe later," I murmured.

"Whenever you're ready," he answered before leaving the room. As he headed downstairs, I wondered if that day would ever come.

Chapter 23

The next day, Mom called again. She'd called several times during the week, but each time, I'd refused to talk to her. Debbie had had her hands full explaining this to our mother. But, no matter how Debbie had pleaded, I hadn't backed down. I knew I couldn't handle hearing Mom's voice, and if I broke down on the phone, she'd probably hop on the first flight out. I didn't want to be the catalyst behind an aborted mission.

This time when our mother called, my sister caught me off-guard with a lie. Something she's never done in her life, which is why I believed her. She was helping me get dressed when the phone rang. Leaning across the bed, she answered, then held the phone out to me.

"Who is it?" I mouthed.

"I have no idea," Debbie replied, looking very innocent.

"Hello?" I said, holding the phone to my ear.

"Teri? Teri, is that you?" my mother asked.

If looks could kill, we would have had to start planning Debbie's funeral. She ignored me and nonchalantly patted me on the head before she left the room.

My mother's voice was tender as she spoke. "Teri, honey, I've been so worried. Do you need me to come home? I'm no good to anyone right now anyway . . . all I can think about is you."

"Mom, I'm fine— " I tried to reassure her.

She wasn't convinced. "Are you sure? You know, you've always been too independent for your own good. But I know you better than you think I do and I . . ."

Giving up, I let her carry on to her heart's content. Debbie and I had learned years ago that we were blessed with an overprotective mother. We were both sheltered from so much, it's a wonder I turned out normal. I share that thought with my sister whenever I feel she's getting too cocky.

" . . . then when Debbie said you were too weak to talk on the phone, I just thought I'd die. I mean, it's bad enough you had to lose your baby, but to not even have your mother there . . ."

I don't think it was so much what she said, but how she said it. The concern in her voice. I knew my mother loved me, and suddenly, I wanted nothing more than to be in her arms.

Debbie had chosen that moment to come back into the room. Sensing I'd had enough, she told the second lie of her life. Taking the phone from my hand, she told Mom we'd call her back, explaining that my blood sugar had dropped and I needed to eat. She hung up the phone, then sat down on the end of the bed.

"I figured Mom would feel better if she could hear your voice for a change," she explained, avoiding my glare. "Edna's waiting downstairs," she added.

"What?"

"Teri, I know you two argued the other day, and I think it would do you both some good to talk it out."

"I don't want to see anyone right now, including you. Besides, I'm not even dressed yet."

"I knew you'd see it my way," she said brightly as she left the room.

"Debbie!" I exclaimed, knowing it wouldn't do any good. Debbie was rebelling big time, breaking every rule I'd ever given her. Frantically, I slid under the covers and reached for the oversized T-shirt Debbie had picked out. Before I could slip it on, Edna appeared in the bedroom door.

"Now, you two stay in here until this is settled," Debbie said firmly. Before either of us could reply, she disappeared downstairs. Eric and Derek, not to mention child number three, were going to be up against some pretty stiff competition in the years to come. I'd never seen my sister this feisty. Maybe pregnancy brought out the best in her.

"I heard about your arm," Edna said, gazing down at the floor.

"Yeah," I replied, still trying to wiggle into the baggy T-shirt.

"Looks like you could use some help," Edna muttered, moving to the bed.

"I can do it," I said stubbornly. I had managed to poke my left hand through the correct sleeve, but was still struggling to get the right sleeve over my cast.

"Here, let me slide that over your head for you," Edna insisted.

I was amazed. The woman was efficient and gentle. Within seconds, the shirt was in place. But when she held up my sweat bottoms, I drew the line.

"I'll get them later," I mumbled, grudgingly thanking her for the help.

She replaced the sweats on the chair and sat down on the side of the bed. "Teri, I'm sorry about the other day. I don't know what got into me. I had no business coming down on you like that."

"I deserved it. It's just . . . I really wanted this baby . . . I can't believe she's gone . . ." The tears I'd suppressed during Mom's call surfaced. Edna quietly gathered me against her, cast and all, and as my mother would have done, rocked me until the dam finally broke.

Chapter 24

Two days later, Mark went with me to see Dr. Moulton. He was as amused over the broken arm as my mother had been.

"You fell on the sidewalk?" He stared quizzically at me. "Why didn't you let me know?"

"I figured the damage was done. Besides, I knew I had to come see you in a few days anyway."

"Don't try to sweet-talk me," he said, a trace of irritation in his voice. "Let's check your blood pressure."

I sat quietly as he pumped up the pressure cuff. As the air hissed out, he smiled. "One twenty-five over eighty . . . couldn't get much better. How do you feel in general?"

"With my hands, generally."

"She's getting her spunk back," Mark added.

"I can see that," Dr. Moulton said dryly. "According to the printout from your monitor, your blood sugar seems to have leveled out . . . which is what we wanted. Everything else seems fine."

"Good. Can we go now?" I asked, eager to leave.

"Actually, there's something I'd like to talk to you and Mark about."

"Oh?" I said, glancing at my husband.

"Teri, I know things didn't turn out the way we'd hoped this time around. Losing your baby three months into the pregnancy was devastating for you . . . for all of us."

I nodded, hoping he wouldn't stir everything up again. I'd shed enough tears the past few days.

"I meant what I told you in the hospital. There will be another chance."

"Yeah, I guess," I sighed.

"You do understand that what happened wasn't your fault?"

"That's what they say."

"Something was wrong with the fetus . . . baby. Dr. Setter called me a couple of times after seeing you. He was concerned because the baby wasn't growing as rapidly as we would've liked."

"I know."

"Would you tell her it didn't have anything to do with the house cleaning she did the day before?" Mark pleaded.

"Teri, you didn't do anything to bring this on. Sometimes, when things aren't right, nature takes over. I know this was the case with you. Next time, I think it will go better."

"What guarantee do I have that it will? I'm not sure I could handle going through this again."

"There are no guarantees, even if a person doesn't have diabetes. In fact, diabetics have the same chance at having a healthy baby as anyone else, if we can keep those blood sugar levels under control."

"Is that really possible?"

Dr. Moulton gazed at me. "It is. In fact, that's what I want to talk to you about."

"Oh?"

"I was going to suggest going with this option before we knew you were pregnant." He reached behind his chair and pulled out a grey plastic briefcase.

"Very nice. Is it new?" I asked, wondering where his fancy leather one was.

"Yes," he replied as he opened the case. I was surprised to see that it was lined with grey foam. He reached inside and pulled out a small, grey square. "This is an insulin pump."

"Really?" Mark said, acting like an excited five-year-old. My husband loves gadgets.

"Really," Dr. Moulton replied. "We've talked about it before and—"

"And I told you then what I'm going to tell you now. No way!"

"Teri . . ."

164

"Didn't you say I'd have to be hooked up to that thing twenty-four hours a day?"

"Yes, although you can be unhooked from it for about an hour . . . if you decide to go swimming, or float a river—"

"Float a river? Are you serious? I've never—"

"You also unhook when you change sites, something you should do about every three days." He smiled at my stern expression. "Believe it or not, some diabetics like it better than the multiple shot therapy."

"I don't care what other diabetics like. I treasure what limited freedom I have with this disease. I don't want to make allowances for anything else."

"Even if it means better control . . . or a chance to get you in better shape for your next pregnancy?"

"I'm not convinced there will be a next pregnancy, okay?! And this I.V. setup gives me the creeps."

"It's not as bad as you think. Once the Sof-set is inserted, only a tiny Teflon canula remains under your skin. Most of our pump patients claim they don't even notice it's in place."

"This is so cool," Mark exclaimed, reaching for the pump. "Where do you store the insulin?"

"In the back. See that tiny compartment?"

Mark turned the pump over in his hands. "Yeah. Can I open it?"

"Sure. That's where you keep a syringe filled with insulin."

"What kind of insulin?" Mark asked. He held it out to me, but I refused to take it.

"Regular. In our climate, it seems to work the best."

"But, isn't that out of her system in a couple of hours? It's the fast-acting insulin, right?"

"Right. That's where the basal rate comes in. It drips in what she needs between meals. And the beauty of it is, we can set several different basal rates for different times. We can program them to fit Teri's schedule."

"Whoa, wait a minute here, I haven't agreed to anything yet."

Dr. Moulton took the pump from Mark and held it out to me. I grudgingly took it from him. "See how light that is?"

I turned it over in my hand. It was lighter than I'd guessed. The small rectangle was about the size of a small beeper. When I mentioned that observation, Dr. Moulton smiled.

"It does resemble a beeper. Especially when you put it inside of this black leather carrying case." He pulled the case out of the grey foam and handed it to me.

It took me a minute to figure it out, but soon I had the pump snug in its carrying case. "So . . . you wear this on a belt, or what?"

"If you want to. Some patients prefer to keep it in a shirt pocket. Some use a clip instead of the case to attach it to pockets, belts . . . they get pretty creative. Two or three of my female patients clip it in their bra. In fact, now there's a special bra pouch on the market for your convenience."

"What?" I asked, my eyes widening.

"That sounds great," Mark said enthusiastically. "She'd have plenty of room to store it there."

Leaning to the side, I punched Mark in the shoulder.

"As for this freedom you're concerned about losing, most pump patients feel they've gained independence with this method."

"How?" I asked skeptically.

"Well, take for instance when you go to a restaurant to eat. Usually you order, then sneak off to a dark corner or the rest room to give your shot because you're too embarrassed to do it in public."

"I don't want to be mistaken for a druggie," I sniffed.

"You're not the only diabetic who feels that way," Dr. Moulton murmured. "With the pump, you place the order, push a few buttons, and the insulin is automatically pumped into your system."

"Wow," Mark said, the look in his eyes saying it all. I knew he wanted one of these to play with. I could tell by the way he was drooling.

"I'll admit, it sounds impressive," I said. "But, what makes you think it will make a difference during a pregnancy?"

"As I've already told you, it's the high blood sugar levels that affect the baby. I've found that in some cases, it's easier to fight those high numbers with a pump than conventional shot therapy. Instead of giving extra shots, you punch in the insulin needed with the pump. And, we can scale the basal rates accordingly. If we find you're running higher at night or during the day, say, in the afternoon, we can program basal rates to combat it."

"It might be a thought," Mark said.

I ignored him and continued to ask questions. Dr. Moulton answered them with such ease, I began getting excited about the idea myself. "So, how long will it take me to get the hang of this?" I finally asked.

Dr. Moulton looked relieved. "I can set you up with our diabetic counselor later this week. She'll spend two or three hours with you, teaching you how to program and operate the pump. We'll want to keep in touch with you for the first few days to make sure you've got it under control. As I already mentioned, the pump is not without its challenges. You'll have to be careful, but I know you can do it."

"What are the risks involved?" Mark asked, looking up from the manual he'd been reading.

"Infection is always a concern, but if she'll stick to our guidelines, it shouldn't be a problem. Also, there's a chance that the canula might bend when it's inserted under the skin. When that happens, the insulin doesn't flow through as it should and the blood sugar level could rise dangerously. That's why we'll have her check those levels at least four to five times a day. If she gets consistently high readings, then we know there's a problem. Other risks . . . in extremely hot weather, the insulin might gel. And, the tubing can get kinked or caught, which again limits the flow of insulin."

"Kinked?" I asked.

"It happens. Most of my patients prefer the 42-inch tubing because the extra length gives them more freedom with site selection and storage. But, it can get twisted into knots, caught in zippers, so on and so forth. Just watch what you're doing when you get dressed each day, and don't bump the canula site. Not only can it inhibit the flow of insulin, but it can also be quite painful. A young lady caught it in her pantyhose one night and ripped it right out."

I winced. "Anything else?"

"Keep batteries with you wherever you go. If they run low,

you'll need to change them immediately."

"How will I know if the batteries need to be changed?"

"An alarm will alert you."

"What kind of an alarm?" I persisted.

"It flashes a message on the tiny screen and beeps three times. If for any reason you aren't getting insulin into your system, it'll continue to beep."

"It beeps?" I asked, lifting an eyebrow.

"The steady beeping means something's wrong. It rarely goes off. The other beeps only sound when you've activated a process, or after a bolus of insulin has successfully been pumped through. While the insulin is dripping in, the pump will click. Something it will also do when it drips in the insulin for the basal rate."

"Clicks and beeps? I'm going to sound like the bionic woman!"

"The clicks are quiet. The people around you won't notice, most of the time. A patient did tell me about the funny looks she got one night at a restaurant. She was dishing up her plate at the salad bar while her pump was clicking in the insulin. When it beeped to announce it was finished, the man standing next to her scurried away to sit in a booth clear across the room. She laughed about it later, convinced he'd thought it was a bomb."

"That doesn't sound very funny," I countered.

"It will," Dr. Moulton promised. "It's important to maintain a sense of humor. One of my patients set off the alarm at the airport as he walked through the metal detector. Another patient wondered why everyone was staring at her in the mall. Her tubing had slipped out and was hanging below her shirt."

"Keep it up and I'm out of here now," I threatened.

"I thought you'd get a kick out of these stories. You'll probably add several more to our collection."

"Maybe."

"Aw, c'mon, Teri, let's try it," Mark pleaded.

Despite everything, I was still leaning toward pump therapy. "Okay. We'll try it for a while. If it doesn't work out, I can always revert back to shots, right?"

"Right," Dr. Moulton agreed. "I really think you're going to like the pump, though. Give it a fair chance and in about six months, maybe we can try another pregnancy."

"Six months?" Mark asked, looking disappointed.

"That's my advice. If we time a pregnancy too close to this last one, she'll be at risk to miscarry again."

"Because of the diabetes?" I asked.

"Not necessarily. Even if you didn't have diabetes, I'd give you the same recommendation. You need to give your body a little T.L.C. before we jump in again. Okay?"

I nodded. I knew it would be long time before I would be ready to *jump in again* emotionally. A very long time.

Chapter 25

It took me several days to get the hang of the insulin pump. Deciding I could use some extra help, I heeded Bishop Anderson's advice and requested a blessing. He was only too happy to help Mark with this endeavor.

Now that I was on the road to recovery, Debbie planned to return home in the near future. As such, I requested that the blessing be administered while she was still here. I thought it would make her feel better about leaving me on my own. And, when Mom called again to see how things were going, it would give us some positive ammo to use.

I was nervous when the bishop arrived. It was tempting to tell him I'd changed my mind. What if this blessing turned into a condemnation? I was certain I'd upset a certain heavenly personage with my attitude and actions since the miscarriage. My faith had teetered on the edge of disbelief. Even now, I found myself wondering about the power of the priesthood. Was it real? I wasn't sure. I still had questions no one had answered, doubts that stubbornly lingered.

Mark picked up on my nervousness and dragged me into the study for a private pep talk. "Teri, I know you're worried about tonight. But, I want you to know something. The priesthood is a wonderful gift given to us from our Heavenly Father. It endows us with the authority to act in His name. The blessings that come through the priesthood power are inspired. Sometimes, we don't always hear what we desire, and sometimes we misunderstand the things that are said. But, always, our Father loves us and He often reveals the very thing we need most to hear."

His testimony touched me, but I still was uncertain.

"We don't have to go through with this," he said quietly. "It's your choice. I think it will help. In fact, I think it will help both of us, but, you decide."

I wanted to cry "foul"; Mark was using my guilt tactic. It was effective—no wonder he always caves in to my requests. As I pondered his advice, my gaze settled on the Sergeant Edna doll sitting near the computer. A surge of love was pricked by guilt. Walking across the room, I picked up the small statue and set it in the waste paper basket on the other side of the desk. It was time to let go of a few misguided perceptions. Time to put my trust in the one person who had never led me astray. "Let's go, Mark," I murmured, taking his hand. "I'm ready."

Chapter 26

The next afternoon, I swung by the grocery store and picked up the biggest container of diet Seven-Up I could find. Then, psyching myself up to do some intensive groveling, I headed for Natalie's house.

Kimberly answered the door. She smiled at me, then hollered for her mother. Natalie walked out of the kitchen, wiping her hands on a dish towel. She motioned for me to come in, and after sending Kimberly off to play with her dolls, joined me in the living room.

"This is for you," I said, setting the liter of pop on the coffee table with my good hand.

"Thanks," she said, her expression indicating she didn't know what to make of it.

"It is your current beverage choice?"

"Yes," she answered, forcing a smile. "Why are you bringing me a gift?"

"Consider it a peace offering."

She lifted an eyebrow, but unfortunately, didn't respond the way I'd anticipated. I'd prepared a speech on the way over. I'd give her the gift. She'd thank me profusely, telling me how thoughtful I was, then I would say she was the thoughtful one and apologize for being such a rat. Natalie had missed her cue.

"You're looking better," she murmured, choosing to sit in the recliner across the room from where I was sitting on the couch. I sensed the distance between us wasn't a good sign.

"I'm feeling better . . . about a lot of things. But, there's still something that isn't quite up to par yet."

"Oh?"

I gazed at Nat. I owed her so much. She'd sensed something wasn't right the day of the miscarriage. Heeding that prompting, she had tried to call me. When there was no answer, she'd called Mark at work. When he'd told her how sick I'd been earlier that morning, she'd hurried over to check things out. She was the one who had called the ambulance, and the one who had very likely saved my life.

"What's wrong?" Natalie asked, puzzled by my silence.

"Us," I replied. "Me, in particular. Nat, I want to apologize for how I've treated you lately. I never meant to hurt you."

She looked down, playing with the dish towel in her hands. "You've always been there for everyone else. Why wouldn't you let us be there for you? Do you know what it would've meant if I'd been able to give back a portion of what you've given me? Instead, you closed a door between us."

I nodded, admitting my guilt. "It's difficult for me to let people in, especially when I'm hurting. Debbie says I'm as stubborn as a clam. I close up tight and bury myself in the sand. It takes quite a bit of prying to open my shell."

"We could try steaming," Natalie said, offering a tiny smile.

Relieved by the implied humor, I relaxed. "Actually, Edna tried that method. She got me so steamed, I couldn't even think straight."

"I heard all about it," she replied, pointing to my cast. "From Edna, and later, from Sylvia Clawson."

I frowned. I hadn't thought about Sylvia. What had Hank told her? I hoped my actions wouldn't dampen her desire to continue coming out to church.

"Don't look so worried. Sylvia's okay about it. I talked to her a couple of days ago at the mall. She wanted to know how you were doing."

"I never dreamed my stupidity could affect so many people."

"You've been through a lot. We understand that."

"Yeah, well, at least this little accident finally jarred me out of self-pity mode," I mumbled, patting my cast.

"You might be interested to know that something else of a positive nature happened."

"Because I broke my arm?" I asked.

"No. Because of the miscarriage. I'll tell you this because I know Gloria never will. You might have noticed she's kept a low profile the past couple of weeks."

I had noticed. Gloria had sent a card, but she hadn't called or come by, which was just as well. Seeing a woman nearly nine months pregnant would've made everything that much harder. Being around Debbie had been hard enough, and she didn't even show yet.

"Gloria stopped to see me a couple of days after you came home. She wanted to see you in person, but felt it wasn't a good idea, considering what you'd been through. Before she left, she said something I think you need to hear."

"Oh?"

"I don't know if you've noticed, but Gloria hasn't seemed very excited about having a baby."

I stared at Natalie. Did anything escape this woman?

"She's dreaded the changes, the sacrifices she and Ian will have to make. Then, when you lost your baby, it put things into perspective for her. She cried while she was here, telling me how horrible she felt. Your loss opened her eyes to how precious life is."

I felt a tear slide down my face. During the blessing last night, I'd been told that my example would influence others for good. That my trials would be a source of strength to those around me. I'd wondered what the bishop . . . the Lord, had meant by that. Now, I was beginning to understand.

"Teri, I didn't mean to make you cry," Natalie said, crossing the room to sit next to me on the couch.

"I know," I sniffed. "There is something you could do for me, though. Something that would help."

"Name it," she said, her eyes dark with concern.

"This," I said as I reached for a hug. We both gasped. Pulling back, I fumbled under my blouse and unhooked the pump from my bra. Then, I reached for Natalie again, determined that nothing would come between us this time.

Epilogue

One year later

There wasn't as much snow on the ground this March, not like last year, which was a good thing, considering the lack of coordination I was experiencing. Those extra few pounds did seem to make a difference. I felt like a walking bowling ball, but didn't mind—most of the time. In nearly two weeks, it would all be over. In two weeks, our baby would be coming out to play, as my husband tactfully put it. Dr. Setter had told us we were expecting another girl, but, I'd cautiously decorated the nursery in mint green and yellow, just to be safe. I didn't want to make Gloria's mistake. She'd been assured her baby was a girl too. Little Shane Hansen had come home wrapped in a pink quilt and had to endure a pink-tinted room the first year of his life.

I should've made a few side bets concerning the outcome of Debbie's pregnancy. She brought home a daughter, a petite towhead named Christine, much to Eric and Derek's disgust. They'd wanted a little brother to torture.

On the other hand, Mom was tickled pink over her first granddaughter. I mean that quite literally. She bought everything in sight that was pink to begin the process of spoilage. Rick, Mark and I weren't much better. Rick gave his daughter the biggest pink teddy bear I've ever seen in my life. Mark and I settled on an assortment of outfits—I couldn't decide which one was the cutest, so we bought them all.

I felt a twinge of sorrow when I held Debbie's baby for the first time. But, it soon passed, giving way to another, more familiar twinge that has lasted most of the past eight months.

I found out last August that Baby Patterson was on his\her way. Dr. Moulton and Dr. Setter weren't very amused; we'd slightly botched our timetable. We really had planned on waiting out the six months before trying again, but, evidently, someone had other plans. He\she gets her impatience from Mark, I'm sure.

Debbie had correctly described the joys of climbing out of a water bed during the eighth month. This morning, that process had to be faced bright and early. Once I was out of bed, with Mark's assistance I might add, I unhooked my pump and made it into the shower. Then, I wrapped a beach towel around myself, waddled back into the bedroom, gazed into my closet, and sighed. Gone were the days when I could pick and choose apparel at whim. I was down to a selection of three outfits that I could still wiggle into. Choosing the fancier one of the three, I began the difficult task of getting dressed.

Edna had told me not to come if I wasn't up to it, but I wouldn't miss this event for the world. I never would've believed it possible, but Emmett and Edna were getting married. Surprisingly, the civil ceremony would take place inside the Idaho Falls Temple. The happy couple had already been sealed to their previous spouses, but had decided they wanted the special atmosphere of the temple to begin their marriage. A reception would be held later at the church.

Mark and I had been invited to the temple ceremony, as had Gloria, Ian, Jerry, and Natalie. We were all riding over to the temple in the new mini-van Natalie and Jerry had purchased last month. With another family member on the way, they had decided they needed some extra room.

I was tickled for Nat. Her baby was due a month after mine, in May. She felt certain she would have a girl. I hoped so. My daughter could use a good friend.

Our presidency had provided wonderful material for several ward jokes. They wanted to rename fourth ward in our honor, calling it "the maternity ward." Or, better yet, christen the Primary end of the building "the nursery wing." To retaliate, we complimented them on their fertile imaginations. But, for the most part, we tried to be good sports, which isn't the easiest thing in the world when your feet hurt, your rib cage feels stretched beyond its normal capacity and you spend most of your time praying to the great white porcelain.

One Sunday, the queasies hit Nat and I at the same unfortunate time. Tight-lipped, we raced to the girls' rest room. Two of the three stalls were occupied. It was rumored later that we fought over the stall that was available, which isn't true. In the excitement of the moment, however, things did get a little crazy. My jumper ripped and Natalie's hair was slightly mussed, but it all worked out. Edna came to the rescue and hustled seventy-five-year-old Margaret Carlisle out of one of the other stalls just in the nick of time. It took us a while to live that one down, but we held our heads up high, and tried to keep our profiles low.

When news leaked out about Emmett's proposal, the pregnancy jokes thrived again, only this time, Edna was the target. She tolerated the good-natured kidding quite well. Evidently, love *is* a many splendored thing. As their relationship blossomed into romance, these two tigers became declawed house cats. Most were stunned by the metamorphosis. I was, with Emmett, but I'd already seen Edna's softer side. In my opinion, Edna was a sweetheart.

The marriage ceremony was a beautiful experience. Through it all, Edna seemed to glow. She had given in to her true hair color this past year and was actually quite attractive with hair as white as the snow outside. As for Emmett, he looked nothing like his former self. Edna's love had transformed him into a very prestigious-looking individual. He was even nice, most of the time. He reverted to his original disposition when Edna's boys came rushing home over Christmas to save their mother from his clutches. Emmett didn't have any problem setting Jake and Ed straight in a big hurry.

It had taken quite an effort, but both boys and their wives were in attendance today. Ed looked uncomfortable in his suit, and Jake's expression was somber, but they were here. It was a start.

I guess that's all any of us ever need when we take a wrong turn in life. A fresh start. A chance to show what we're really made of. An opportunity to exhibit faith when nothing seems certain.

That's when we truly begin to grow as individuals . . . and when we finally realize we don't always need to see the fine print.

Author's Note

When *Kate's Turn* came out last year, several people wanted to know if I had based the story on my life. I'm anticipating similar questions with this book. For the record, both Kate and Teri are figments of my imagination. As with most writers, I draw on past experiences to some degree. I observe those around me and, at times, pattern some of my characters after their example, using creativity and research to flesh out the rest of the story.

To be truthful, I do have a few things in common with Teri. I am a diabetic and I have a wonderful husband who is very supportive. Friends who know me well have said that there are other similarities between Teri and me. I'm still not speaking to them. (Kidding!!) This novel does portray a character close to my heart. I hope that when people read it, they will gain an insight into what it is like living with a chronic illness.

Regardless of what I may have thought in the beginning, diabetes is not a four-letter word, although some may see it as a curse. I'll never deny that it's a challenge, but on the bright side, it has provided opportunities for growth and has taught me to appreciate the moment at hand. As with many things, attitude is everything. (I have to give credit to a former Mia Maid of mine, Heidi Burdick, for that helpful reminder.) Annoying though the thought may be, it is true. I've talked to diabetics who don't care, who don't hope. Their philosophy scares me, because they're the ones who usually end up with complications. They give up, thinking it will never get any better.

In this novel, I mentioned that living with diabetes is like walking a tight rope. This is an accurate description. But, despite what most people think, balance can be achieved. It's not easy, the control may not always be perfect, but diabetes is a livable condition. And, there is always hope.

I've been on the insulin pump for nearly four years and love it. It's not without its challenges, but to me, it's worth it. I've had several adventures similar to those described in this novel. But I feel as though I've been given my life back. I'm no longer on set schedules. Participating in sports is easier. I even play city-league volleyball.

Living with diabetes in today's world isn't as bad as one might think. New discoveries and products are constantly being made available that make it easier and better. Dedicated research makes this possible. We've been promised that a cure is on the horizon. If we can keep from developing complications while we wait, eventually a new life will be waiting for us—a life free of insulin shots, pumps, oral medications, and diets. It's this message of hope that the ADA (American Diabetes Association) promotes.

A good friend of mine, Denise Kallstrom, and I feel so strongly about this message that four years ago, we put together the Bear Lake County chapter of the ADA. We get together in our support group and try to convince other diabetics that life isn't so bad. We don't always succeed, but once in a while our excitement rubs off on someone else. We've seen lives change, including our own. Denise has a healthy daughter now, because of the tight control method. As for myself, I have three sons. I've also had every test they've ever come up with for diabetic complications, and I've passed them all with flying colors. It's a constant battle, but one that is definitely worth it.

This past year, I was invited to speak at a couple of the local schools concerning diabetes. A teacher commented later that I have "a bubbly outlook on life." She went on to say that if a person didn't know me, they'd never guess I have diabetes. I'd like to set the record straight here. Being a diabetic doesn't necessarily go hand in hand with having an attitude problem. Many diabetics are very sweet, even-tempered individuals. We may even be a little spunky on occasion, but that's a good thing. That's how we survive in a world that doesn't always understand how it is to live with a chronic illness. Another teacher mentioned that it appears I pretty much lead a normal life—the diabetes doesn't stop me. He's right. I hope it never will.

Cheri J. Crane

P.S. If you have any questions concerning the DCCT (Diabetes Control & Complications Trial), insulin pump therapy, or diabetes in general, look for a clinic or an internist who is up on the latest diabetic research, or contact the local American Diabetes Association (ADA) affiliate, which is usually listed in the phone book. Or contact the head ADA office at the American Diabetes Association, 1660 Duke Street, Alexandria, VA 22314 (703) 549-1500, Ext. 312.

About the Author

Music, sports, community and church service, and lots of family time can't seem to keep Cheri Nel Jackson Crane from writing. Cheri also plays guitar and piano by ear, writes songs, loves racquetball, baseball, and volleyball, and she enjoys cooking. She currently serves in her ward Young Women's presidency and heads a local chapter of the American Diabetes Association

Author of the best-selling *Kate's Turn*, Cheri Crane is a former resident of Ashton, Idaho. She and her husband, Kennon, live in Bennington, Idaho, with their three sons. *The Fine Print* is Cheri's second novel.